A Flash of Darkness

Collected Stories of

M. M. De Voe

Borda Books
Santa Barbara, CA, 93105, U.S.A.
www.bordabooks.com

ISBN: 979-8-9879269-0-1

Copyright © 2023
Library of Congress Control Number: 2023904047

" [It] actually doesn't matter what I feel. What matters is how the art makes you feel."

—Margaret Atwood

Collection Curator: Max Talley
Designed and edited by Angela Borda
Assistant Editor: Maryanne Knight

Previously published stories in this collection

Baltimore Review: "The Scissors of Hope and Despair"
The Brooklyn Rail: "Tastemakers"
BuzzyMag: "Cineplex"
Delirium Corridor Anthology: "Left Brain"
Fickle Muses: "From the Leaf Lore"
Literal Latte: "Virgin Flight 244, Chicago to Heathrow" (1st place winner)
Lithuania In Her Own Words, a PEN anthology: "A Rose"
New Millennium Writings: "Empty" (1st place award)
Santa Barbara Literary Journal: "The Mayor of Flashback," "Shutter"
Stone Voices: A Journal for the Visual Arts: "Leave Me"
Stand Out, The Best of the Red Penguin Collection: "Big Bad"
Twisted Book of Shadows Anthology: "Cake"

Table of Contents

Curator's Foreword..9

Shutter..13

Tastemakers..21

Still Life with Summer Cherries........................29

The Mayor of Flashback.....................................41

The Scissors of Hope and Despair....................59

Mom of the Year..77

Decorated..99

Wild Witch Treats...111

Empty...125

Cineplex...129

Leave Me...147

Left Brain..163

Money in the Bank..177

Cake...183

From the Leaf Lore...195

TOC Continued

Big Bad..215

A Rose 227

Virgin Flight 244, Chicago to Heathrow................247

Acknowledgements..250

Biography..251

foreword

Collection Curator is not a standard designation. I was essentially the acquisition editor for this project. But what I sought to acquire for Borda Books was not a specific manuscript or story, but the author herself, M. M. De Voe. I knew she had written fiction for over twenty years, in a variety of genres. Inquiries were made; interest was bruited about. The air filled with chatter. However, the initial collection she submitted got turned aside. Not so much rejected as to provoke genuflecting, followed by, "We are not worthy." It was well-written literary fiction that absolutely deserved to be published. By normal, sane publishers.

What I wanted was De Voe's most intense writing. The fearless stuff, the "I'm not sure my family should read this" type of fiction. We could call it speculative or genre fiction, but it's really psychological fiction. The characters all have some bizarre things going on in their minds. What is real and what is unreal? Who are the reliable narrators and who are inglorious charlatans?

After some delicate "We love you, but..." communications, De Voe sent in a collection of the odd, the dark, the challenging. Stories that ranged from 2005 to the present (though one may originate from the late '90s). Many had been published by the smarter literary journals and anthologies of our time. At that point, my curating job became easy. A matter of fiddling with the story order to achieve some hard-to-define sense of balance, of subtracting a couple of tales and requesting one or two more be added. This process went rapidly and seemed generally mirthful.

My editorial belief is that if you must do substantial story editing or ask an author for major rewrites of their work, you have failed in both your acquisition and curatorial duties. You picked the wrong person. Luckily, I didn't. So, having done minimal requisite fixes, I can sit back and present *A Flash of Darkness,* a story collection that contains multitudes. De Voe juggles literary fiction with fables, science fiction with horror, pagan satire with the fantastical. But what shines through is intelligence and daring. The ability to write from the point of view of a variety of narrators—some worthy, even heroic, others flawed to the extreme.

Dive in to the haunted atmosphere of "Shutter," as we linger on the outskirts of horror past or horror-to-be. "Tastemakers" satirizes a modern obsession with life as performance art. "The Mayor of Flashback" is pure literary fiction that intertwines memories of 9/11 in Manhattan, Russian escapades, and the sometimes elastic bonds of marriage. "Empty" takes us into a corporate Twilight Zone, while "Cake" is a frightening peek into a domestic world, where keeping an eye on the children may not necessarily be for *their* safety. Toward the end, "A Rose" delivers a knockout punch of shifting fables and narrators that shows in a single story what this author's imagination can accomplish.

Did anyone get a trifle vexed when their suggested collection title, *First I Killed Your Houseplants,* wasn't used? Ask me in twenty years when I recover. M. M. De Voe did a fantastic job creating these stories and Angela Borda continues her winning streak at editing and design. I basically rode along in the motorcycle's sidecar and said, "Keep going. This is fun!"

—Max Talley
Collection Curator
Author of *My Secret Place* and *Santa Fe Psychosis*

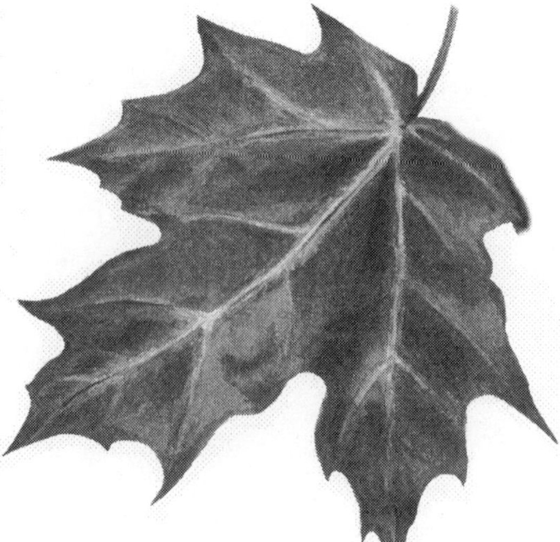

Shutter

The young woman chose the bench beneath the only maple tree, a tree stunted by lack of light. This tree may remind her subliminally of home. She has the plain, craggy facial structure of a New England girl, born in an antique-cluttered village by a lake, transported by proudly still-married parents to the big city for college. Now all of that is far behind her. Nothing practical left. Her little black dress shows some waist and some hip through star-shaped cutouts, the dress is eveningwear, probably expensive—even though it's mid-afternoon, even though she works at a rotten barista job. From this vantage, I can't see her feet, only her face and torso. Her eyeliner sparkles gold; rather much for a job that chiefly involves steamed milk and an iPad. A passing dog barks at a curious squirrel and she smiles. A pretty smile. A youthful smile. Naïve. She's the type who thinks bad things happen only to people who don't try hard enough. She wears an eternally hopeful expression. She has to be an actress or a model—or believes she will be soon. She looks like I used to look. I drew a mean cappuccino, met the eyes of my customers, glared at the condescending ones, winked at the cute ones, searched always for my big lucky break.

Not anymore.

The young woman sits alone on the park bench enjoying the rust-toned rainbow of autumn leaves decorating this crisp but gray October afternoon when the old guy approaches. I watch through the branches. I know what's next. The guy looks harmless, a laughable caricature of the successful older gentleman. Shiny teeth, bouffant black hair, deep tan. I see through him; she is too young for the x-ray vision of age. The teeth are false, the hair is implanted and dyed, the tan owes more to lamps than beaches. Iron-tipped cane? Genuine—but more weapon than affectation. The piercing eyes have seen too much yet remain eager to see more. That's attractive, in its way. Like an echo of a song that got stuck in your head once when you were doing something risky and foolish.

She can't be more than twenty, a college kid working extra shifts to pay for audition shoes. Not a thought past next month's rent.

"Mind if I sit here?" he says, startling her into looking at him. Strangers don't usually talk to you in a city. This man is a few generations beyond her interest level, so she ignores him. Not a prospective mate, not a friend, not a threat. She's wrong about the last one. I move to get a better vantage.

The shoes. Pink toenails peep from gold straps. Gem-encrusted stiletto heels after the fashion of the hour. Accessories like that cost more than their asking price. I should know.

Leaves scatter at her feet. The brown sighs of spent beauty. Her legs move restlessly. I can hear the insistent shush of the leaves she disturbs, a supernatural warning she won't heed.

He asks again. Polite. Persistent. "Perhaps you didn't hear me. Would you mind if I sat down?"

"Not at all," she quickly replies, her sudden blush because she fears the old gentleman will think her rude. Like all young people, far too worried about their image in the eyes of others. "Of course. Please. Sit."

The old-school manners her doting parents taught her: he twists them into an opportunity.

She scoots over on the long bench. The older man slides into the wide space, leaving enough room for a third person, but on the wrong side of himself.

I don't interfere. Yet.

Barely two minutes pass. They watch a burble of pigeons battling an aggressive sparrow. They look at their phones. He checks a stock price. She giggles at Instagram: a sepia-filtered close-up of long-lashed Asian eyes peeking over a brimming glass of wine. She clicks the heart. Sighs happily. Lowers her phone. Picks it up to check the time. Her neighbor leans into her as if about to reveal a secret or tell an off-color joke. He points at her feet.

"What color do they call that?"

It's the line he always uses. I had just had my very first pedicure. I was eighteen. That was fifteen years ago. I haven't aged. I never will age. I died in his studio. He took pictures.

Before and after.

She looks at her manicured toes. "Pink," she says, dryly. Girls are smarter now. Smarter but still naïve.

He gets her joke. Leans back. Laughs. There's a bit of Cary Grant about it. A bit of Gregory Peck. He's that old. But still fit. Still spry, they would say. He still has it. His spine is not curved as one would expect from a man with a cane. The cane breathes money but hides weaponry. The overly sweet drink he will offer her upstairs will be drugged. His eyes are sharp. His hands look particularly strong. He drags from a cigarette I hadn't noticed. Smoking is new for him. I wonder what it hides. He exhales hard, keeping the stream of smoke away from the young woman, blowing it towards the empty seat on the bench. My seat, though I don't take it. She looks grateful for the consideration. That's bad. She sees him as a nice guy. He's not.

"Yeah, I know it's pink," he says. "But what do they call it?"

There is a moment when I think she will elude him. She hesitates as if debating whether to tell this old dude to get the hell away from her. But instead she laughs and blushes.

"Pink-a-boo, actually."

He laughs. Repeats the name. She is warming to him. I consider my options. There isn't much I can do; I know this from past experience. They trust nothing, these girls, except compliments. And bad guys feed them excellent compliments.

"That's nice," he says, "Real nice. You from Brooklyn? The Bronx?"

"No," she replies. I can tell from her tone a doubt has crossed her mind. She's wondering suddenly how she has come to be in conversation with this guy. When he stubs out his cigarette, the smell of his smoke is replaced by something altogether more sour. Age. Knowledge. Intent. She doesn't notice, but I feel dizzy. It's now or never.

"Well, you seem tough. I like a fierce young woman. You an actress?"

"Why? Are you a producer?"

"Matter of fact." He leans back. "I am."

"Really?"

"Really."

They both notice the crazy rustling leaves. The maple shakes like a storm is coming. The other trees are still. The sky is a thick gray blanket, motionless. Not a breath of wind rustles a blade of grass. The clouds don't move. The tree branches flail. It's weird. A warning. A sign.

Unfortunately, the shared experience draws her closer to him.

"That was weird."

"There must be a wind eddy here. Or something. Anyway. Yeah. I'm a producer. And I like your look."

I shake the tree again, but to no avail. He has won again. Over and over, he wins. Twice in the last fifteen years. A careful five-year schedule of unsolvable atrocities.

"You're putting me on."

"Here's my card, sweetheart. I'm the real deal. My studio is just upstairs. Let me buy you a drink."

"Right now?"

"Sure, why not?"

"I'm in the middle of a shift."

"They won't miss you." He grins. "This is the city. People come and go."

My ghost can only warn her as I tried to do for the two others. I care, but I am not responsible. Those young women are haunting spots more meaningful to them. A medical student and a waitress. All wannabe models. Is there a girl in the world who doesn't wish someone would say she is perfect, exactly as she is? There is nothing more I can do. I shake the branches and hope. And pray. The young woman tilts her head as if she hears something funny.

"Wait just a minute," she says, and bites a dry flake from her lower lip. Her hands smooth her hair. There is no wind. The tree showers her with leaves that have died too quickly to fall on their own. Her forehead furrows. She looks for the bird, the squirrel—sees only autumn branches. Only the brassy beauty of the nearly dead.

He looks at his oversized diver's watch, reminding her he holds a promise of wealth, but that the offer is fleeting. He beckons her with the hand holding the lit cigarette. The hot ember traces what could be a magic sigil, some sort of bewitchment. Some violence against nature.

"Come up. Do you think I'm going to hurt you? Do I look like I could?"

She laughs, sure of her own strength. Too shrewd to be taken in.

The young are so confident in their abilities. She fingers the soft, thick card in her hand, rubs her thumb across the black letters. What is her experience with business cards? To her the ecru cardstock probably seems professional. She is used to screens, social media, and video chats; she's unfamiliar with the feel of embossed paper. She relies on the safety of typeface, the factuality of names and numbers. She hasn't yet learned that everything she can touch might also be a lie. To distract her from the textured card, I shake the leaves again, but I recognize the moment when hope expands to fill the gaps in her trust. She runs a finger over the centered word PRODUCER as if it is a musky, pheromone-laced scent to sample in a glossy magazine.

"What do you say? Come up, check out the scene? You can leave in a heartbeat if you think it feels wrong. I happen to need a girl with exactly your coloring for my next project. Kismet. Do kids your age still say kismet? Fate. It's pure fate. We'll do a screen test. Take a few photographs. Celebrate with a daytime drink after. You have my card."

The sun bursts through the gray, and the rustling maple leaves explode orange.

A girl with pink toenails laughs off the predator who offered to ply her with drinks in the middle of the day. In the harsh sunlight she can see right through him. She snaps a photo of his old-school pose, leaning on the cane in a manner that once upon a time might have been considered alluring, dangling the type of cancer-causing cigarette no one in their right mind smokes anymore. His old age is framed by orange leaves, his predatory gaze highlighted by the small splash of blue sky. She posts the shot to Instagram, #creepyoldman, #escape, #yikes, sees the time, and runs off to finish her shift at the coffee shop.

The old man looks after her. Makes that sucking, clicking tsk with his tongue against his front teeth, the same disappointed sound he makes once their pulses still, filling that infinitesimal moment it takes for a ghost to float free of its beautiful spent body, filling that second before he stops the camera and starts the tedious cleanup. The nervous habit shakes his upper dentures loose. He looks furtively around, hastily presses them upward against his gums. Smacks his lips, put-together again. He thinks he was unseen, thinks he is still as invincible as he was at thirty, but this won't go on forever. His knees creak when he pushes against cane and gravity to rise to his feet, and he grunts in discomfort. His body is in decay, and when it fails, his ghost will meet mine. Meanwhile, I'm biding my time. Frustrating his plans. I'm planning to take away his toys one by one.

I curl up in the leaves, windmill seeds for my pillow, gathering my reserves.

Tastemakers

The museum is quiet. Still as statues, the two face each other across the chasm, a Calder dangling between them, curved white walls studded with abstract art at their backs. The ghost of Frank Lloyd Wright cringes against the massive skylight, worried his seminal structure might finally be upstaged, but no one takes any notice of him.

Kit Watanabe, the half-Asian illustrator, looks down eight floors. Her black hair falls around her face like the final curtain of an opera no one has ever enjoyed. In her mind, a media loop features a sports commentator from the Olympics. She imagines the gray-haired diving champ telling the TV audience about her wealthy-yet-indifferent banker husband and her artistic frustrations as a professional illustrator. She imagines her own much-younger face on YouTube as she sneers, "I don't do kids' books." That might have been the turning point of her career. Her manicured nails drum the waist-high wall of the Guggenheim. She has scripted everything, down to her nail color.

Across the void, Manuel Garcia's eyes take up the hunt. His British boyfriend, in a meth frenzy, had slashed every one of Manuel's paintings to ribbons. The gallery in Chelsea was sorry for his loss, but needed to show something. So Manuel Garcia broke up with the drug addict and constructed an ironic papier-mâché cast of an enormous bowler hat from the remains of his art. Unable to find a buyer interested in the sculpture before his rent was due, Manuel, once voted "Most Likely to Succeed," looks up at the star-shaped skylight, then back to the ground floor.

Garcia and Watanabe eventually find what they seek: a tourist has set his camera flat on the floor of the Guggenheim, facing up the spiral to the ovoid ceiling. The red light indicates that a timer has been set. It flashes.

Flashes.

Then flashes double-time. Kit's chin bobs, once. Sharp.

"One two three go," Manuel says in a quiet, quick voice without a breath or a pause. He has no discernible accent. At the signal, their feet leave the floor. They push up to perfectly mirrored handstands on the low curved wall.

***

One two three go. Synchronized divers used this phrase

during the 2016 Summer Olympics. On their fifth round of drinks at Prohibition, a dive jazz club on the Upper West Side of Manhattan, while synchronized divers tumbled on six screens over the bar, Kit and Manuel proposed a sloppy toast to the artistic emptiness in their lives. Their pint glasses clattered together in an elevated kiss and briefly blocked the televised image of two young Swedes freefalling in beautiful tandem.

"Fuck," said the bartender (who was trying to watch the television). She had full-body tats, as if she'd rolled naked across the comic pages of a wet newspaper. "They work so hard, and for what? Who comes up with these stupid events and gets people to train their whole lives for three minutes of competition? What good does this skill do in real life?"

"That's us," Manuel muttered into his beer. Kit laughed herself off the barstool and had to work to convince the bartender she was sober enough for another lager.

The seed was planted. They trained every day at their local Equinox until they could hold side-by-side handstands and perfectly invert them into tandem walkovers within four seconds.

They estimated 1.4 seconds to perform the remainder of their piece.

Kit chose this exhibit, Tastemakers, as the perfect backdrop for their performance.

"It's thrown together, but getting great reviews," she had said.

It is the closing day of the exhibit, and the spiral ramp is thronged.

Tourists notice the mirrored double handstand and are amused. Children first, adults later, pointing, assuming it is a show.

It is.

Manuel Garcia is wearing gray Bermuda shorts and a Ralph Lauren polo shirt, but an old one, where the logo is too small to easily identify. Kit Watanabe wears matching gray: a mini-skirt that flutters around her long waist while her City Midnight hair sweeps the white railing, adding points to the artistic portion of the program. She has also chosen Ralph Lauren, though her logo is huge, possibly to call attention to her breasts one final time. Her arms tremble a bit.

The guards look for guidance. One hand moves to a walkie-talkie, another looks to a docent who is still explaining a sculpture installation to a group of Germans. One of the Germans takes a photo of the beige sunglasses on the docent's head, missing the better show behind him. Still, the photograph will eventually be blown up until Kit's extended foot is visible in the reflection of the glasses. The photograph will win an award. Of course.

In his half of the perfectly executed double handstand, Manuel's back is to Kit, and in his sightline now is Emilio Vedova's *Image of Time (Barrier)*. Angular, graphic strokes of black paint on a white canvas, accented by slashes of yellow and orange-red. He has never liked it. In the last conscious thought about art that he will ever have, Manuel realizes that he actually prefers this piece upside down.

In tandem, their bodies arch over the railing, their spines

curve and now their feet lead them through space.

***

When they tuck their knees quickly to complete the dive, the spectators all gasp. Watanabe and Garcia—abdominal muscles tensing as they spin—two full rotations and then a twist and look at that extension!

The tourist's camera on the floor of the Guggenheim flashes, immortalizing the moment.

People scream and leap out of the way. The divers' arms sweep out to their sides and then behind their torsos in perfect butterfly harmony.

People are still screaming. Still scrambling. Her head smashes to the cement one one-hundredth of a second earlier than his, but the snaps of their necks and spines, the crumple of bone against floor, their iPhones' crystal displays cracking—all this happens as one. No one notices the speck of extra red on the Jackson Pollack at the foot of the spiral except the ghost of Frank Lloyd Wright. Watanabe and Garcia have made a permanent mark on his Guggenheim. The guards have leaped into action too late.

***

On an instant replay, you would have seen Kit's brief, satisfied smile. Manuel also would look pleased, though his legs were not entirely tight; his toes in his black leather Kenneth

Coles not entirely pointed. Really, the team could have choreographed this better, but no one is videotaping this event. This will be their first and only run.

Garcia had his troubles with the drug-addicted boyfriend and thought he would never be out of debt, commentators will speculate later. Happily married Watanabe was wealthy by middle-American standards; perhaps this is why, before today, no one has ever taken her art seriously.

But now—!

The Guggenheim guards place "no photographs" signs beside the roped-off bodies, as if the grisly aftermath of this performance is a special exhibit.

***

In the morning, the preprogrammed Tweets begin.

They always arrive at 9:12 am. Fans following #SynchronizedSuicide speculate that the numbers represent a date of importance, a birthday or anniversary. The only people who could explain it are dead.

The Tweets appear simultaneously, on separate feeds. This too, is noted in the chatter.

Day 1—Yesterday was a good day to die.
#synchronizedsuicide

Day 2—Kind of reconsidering the whole death thing.
#synchronizedsuicide

Day 3—Afterlife sucks.
#synchronizedsuicide

Day 4—What are the papers saying about me?
#synchronizedsuicide

Day 5—Here's a link to my Kickstarter campaign to fund #synchronizedsuicide

By Day 25, the Kickstarter has crowdsourced enough money to fund another pair of young artists. The biggest donors get an e-mail saying where they should go to watch. The two fellowship winners, randomly selected from the pool of applicants, are a sculptor who was turned down for six NEA grant cycles, and a digital photographer whose last show was sparsely attended and poorly reviewed.

The pair train daily in the Palladium Athletic Facility at NYU. They are scheduled to jump off the roof of the Met in early spring. Human Rights groups argue back and forth whether this should be allowed. The hashtag has followers in the tens of thousands. Someone has made a Facebook page. Garcia and Watanabe have made it. Six months after their deaths, like Frank Lloyd Wright and his famous museum, they have become polarizing cocktail conversation. They are tastemakers. They will endure.

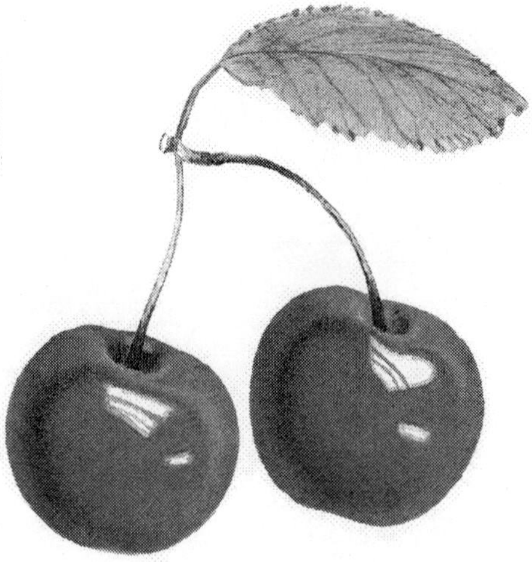

Still Life with Summer Cherries

The heat and humidity of that summer poisoned the air. My open window gave no relief, inviting in garbage smells from the so-called courtyard, along with sounds of trapped dogs whining for cooler air. The sunlight that hit the window from noon to 1 p.m. contained more torture than poetry. The unnamed neighborhood between Chinatown and the East River was, as always, devoid of tourists, devoid of taxis, devoid of anything but transients and the sad people, like me, who lived here.

Across the central shaftway, its shadowy floor paved with cracked cement, mismatched folding chairs, and garbage rather than a postage stamp of grass or a tiny community garden for the tenements on our block, cherries had arrived on the opposite windowsill, so firm and juicy, just looking at the brimming bowl made me long for meaningless kisses in a deserted orchard overgrown with weeds, a tractor rusting in front of a dull barn, the buzz of insects threatening to invade my burnt and peeling skin. As I drowned in syrupy memories of knees sinking into hot, wet loam, sticky cotton, vanilla ice-cream kisses, furtive glances at the distant clouds threatening storms, and all the other ingredients of swift, cloying summer love, a long-dormant hunger woke, but it was too hot to act. I just watched the window.

It is possible I used a telescope.

It started with tiny flies flickering around the bowl of cherries. When they first appeared, the fruit flies were just fragments of specks crossing the lens, barely recognizable as insects, invisible unless one of them happened to angle across the fruit just so. But after a while there were more of them, many more, like a translucent heat shimmer, moving so quickly I could not make out any one individually; a cloud of tiny wisps of insect life.

For days I sat at my window on and off, smiling, focused only on the bowl on the windowsill. I was usually talking to Taylor on my old iPhone—I couldn't afford an upgrade, not with what I earned in hospitality—and while I pretended to listen to complaints about the annoying people where Taylor worked, what I cared about was the meaning of the bowl, given my neighbor's situation. Was it a coincidence or was this an invitation? Perhaps it was mockery? Or a threat? I rehashed the details of our summer fling while watching the flies breed and swarm.

I wanted only to know why I had been dumped. Yes, it was a summer fling, I knew that. But why cut off all communication? I wanted to know. I needed to know. It was why I hadn't accepted the tempting invitation of the cherries, and why even so, I could not stop watching. Even when it became perfectly clear no one would ever explain that gorgeous summer to me. Would not. Could not.

First one perfect cherry turned gray near the stem, then the adjacent one, and so forth until all of the beautiful dark cherries had tasted rot under the assault of the dust-like flies. The body remained lying nearby on the thick dirty carpet, arms thrown overhead as if to ward off the darkness. A book was face down; placed this way to mark the page that needed further studying. The cherries slowly went soft from within, each dark surface losing its delicate tension as the purple skin deepened and crumpled at crease and stem, while the small flies flitted in and out of the sunlight let in by the half-lowered shade over the open window.

I kept watching, numb, with Taylor nattering in my ear about job, goals, coworkers, commute, our upcoming dates, sometimes canceling, sometimes looking forward to them, sometimes remembering something I had said that sounded weird, something I had done that seemed off, worrying about me, but always returning to job, coworkers, commute, stress, pressure, until the whole bowl of cherries had turned from something that made me want more, to something that made me reject what I already had.

No one ever threw the cherries away. My poor neighbor couldn't, of course, and no one else ever came. The book had a pentagram on the back cover, though it was angled so I couldn't make out the title, even through the telescope. It was an old book, one of those with pages that needed to be cut apart with a knife. My neighbor really liked that kind of weird shit. I remember wending through antique stores as a couple, laughing at how cool the morbid stuff was.

Sirens like fingernails skittering across a far-off chalkboard screeched across the distant parts of the city where neighbors looked out for each other. That summer, the one of the fling, had also been particularly hot, and fires were constantly breaking out in places where there were still nice things to burn. There had been sirens then too.

I had eagerly accepted the invitation to go upstate. To the country. To a cherry orchard. With a stranger. A person whose name I didn't even know. It was a summer wildness, born of an overheated brain, too many hours in threadbare silk that stuck uncomfortably in the sweaty folds of my skin. In this neighborhood there was nothing to be done about the leaden heat, no air conditioning, no one had the energy even to open a fire hydrant. Sometimes, people who had paid their ConEd bills would stick their faces in an open freezer, until one of their many squatter roommates objected to either the smell or the expense. These objections were never peaceful or quiet. They usually involved loud cursing, often in multiple languages. Sometimes an otherwise beloved pet would squeal in pain as it got underfoot. Sometimes a child. This neighborhood was no different from the bowl of cherries placed on the sill, cherries that slowly moldered, attracting the lowest kinds of life, which caused the rotting process to accelerate.

The distant sirens made me aware that I should do something for my gorgeous lover, in payment for giving me the best memories of my life, but that time had already passed. The questions would be impossible. Even Taylor wouldn't understand why I had waited, what could make me listen blandly to stories of work and commute and not say something about my neighbor, who had been lying on the floor for days now. How would that particular call go? How could I tell emergency workers that nothing was natural over there? And our relationship? I wasn't sure that I hadn't been bewitched that summer; how was I supposed to explain the heedless, hedonistic joy? Anything I said would implicate me. They would say it was retribution for the breakup. My gorgeous neighbor was, in any case, beyond help. I continued to sit at the window and listen to Taylor who was perfectly normal and in summer happiness mode—talking music, blockbuster movies, recipes for peach pie, margaritas with roasted mango, rooftop parties—while I watched.

Needless to say, I had not invited Taylor over for a long while. I blamed it on the lack of A/C.

Ants came. Marching with incredible precision and potent chemical trails up the pockmarked brick wall and across the peeling white paint to the bowl of decayed fruit. These ants were no monsters; they were dashes of black far too tiny to do more than tear away small pieces of the empurpled skin of the cherries, sawing away with their tiny strong mandibles, releasing overripe rotting scents into the dank air that sometimes carried across the narrow breezeway into my apartment. They left the body alone.

Ants, with their super strength and incredible tenacity, their long, determined journeys and intricate societal structures have always thrilled me. Who hasn't known since childhood that one little ant can lift its own weight a hundred times over? If only humans could carry their own weight… These were ordinary house ants that didn't even bite unless provoked. They were after the sugar in the decomposing fruit; it was nature, just nature. Impressive that they had managed to get up to the fifth floor walk-up but they were still just ants. The colony probably lived under the building's back stoop. The fine black line followed the straight edge of the sill so that if you were not specifically looking for the line of marching insects, you probably would not even have seen it. They made no dent to the bowl of cherries. If anything, it looked like these particular ants were being polite, and leaving the lion's share for someone else.

It must have been the smell that eventually brought the rodents. To be fair, the maggots got there first, but who notices maggots? No one can look at them long, the way they have neither discernible head nor tail, enough like bright white grains of rice that at first you think your eyes are tricking you and that the scattered rice is just rice, though it looks very strange. It can't possibly be moving. You tell yourself it's the terrible stench that keeps wafting from that apartment into yours that's making your eyes swim, and it's only later while you are gagging and gasping and needing to refocus the telescope several times that it hits you that those white spots are indeed maggots and that they are absolutely moving. How they wriggle throughout the meat, writhing; yet they remain an unlikely shade of toothy white; tiny and squirmy beings, never still when they feed. They are too clean for the task that they have evolved to do.

I don't like maggots.

The point is, that while the maggots arrived long before the rodents, it was at last the rodents swarming up and down the side of the building that brought the state of things to a place that warranted putting Taylor on hold and calling the police to tell them that I thought maybe someone across the shaftway needed help because rats were swarming in through the open window and could someone please, please do something quickly.

They came.

It was a few hours later, since no one is in much of a rush these days, particularly in that neighborhood in New York City. But the distinctive wail of the NYPD siren alerted me that it was a squad car. I think I was expecting a fire truck or an ambulance. I crammed the cheap telescope back into the closet and returned to the window, pulling the crappy blinds up all the way. I figured it was something that any curious neighbor might do, stare at police action across a shaftway. The fat Dominican who served as that building's illegal super entered the room first, and a grim police lady went second, and a big cop went third because, as he told the other two in a velvety bass copvoice that easily carried across to my window, although he had a very strong stomach for crime he was pretty terrible around vermin, and he especially hated rats after that thing he'd seen after Sandy. There was a thick silence then, and Taylor jabbering about *discrimination, boss, unfair* until I couldn't see straight and gasped out, "I've been listening to your fucking job stuff nonstop since we first hooked up, and it's time for me to talk for a while, because shit is going down in a big way."

Taylor stopped talking.

Panting a little, I described what I could see. The Dominican super removed the rotting bowl of cherries from the windowsill and lowered the blinds one-handed. Just before they closed, the room seemed to go dark. Then I heard the big cop cursing in his deep voice, followed by a dreadful thud, and then the lady cop shrieked and there was a smaller but no less awful thud.

Taylor, it turned out, was a good listener.

I heard the superintendent shouting Spanish prayers and curses, approaching the window. The shade buckled out as his body fell against it, as if he had been trying to jump but had been stopped, and when the shade tore off, I could see the super was still holding the bowl of cherries. He collapsed, and his screaming abruptly stopped as the bowl fell with him to the floor. Putrid cherries chuckled out in all directions and the few that still held their form rolled into corners and bounced under the furniture. The superintendent did not move again.

Flies swarmed the new bodies.

I fell silent, absorbed in watching the flies gather.

Taylor begged me to keep talking.

I came to myself. The big cop and the lady cop lay in twisted agony near my neighbor's body. They were all lifeless. Taylor kept asking what had happened and I kept giving the same answer.

"I didn't see it happen," I said, "A flash of darkness. That's all I saw. Then the shade was torn off and they were all dead."

"But how? What killed them?" Taylor asked.

"I'm telling you, aren't I? It looked like a flash of light swept the room, only if that flash was made of darkness. A flash of darkness," I said. I repeated the phrase a third time, and Taylor whimpered like a victim in a Japanese anime. But I was the one that needed to be afraid. I was the one that had seen it. "Stay on the phone," I begged, cowering with only my eyes over the windowsill, cupping my headphone mic close to my lips. Taylor tried to switch to FaceTime but I was suddenly afraid we would not be able to reconnect, and then I would be alone in my apartment, one shaftway's distance from whatever that darkness had been.

Taylor kept telling me to calm down and after a while even made jokes, like suggesting we list the apartment as an Airbnb since there wasn't anyone around anymore to stop us. I didn't laugh. I stared at the corpses across the shaftway and had the fleeting thought that maybe Taylor wasn't a keeper.

***

But in times of intense fear, any human connection is enough to keep you tethered to your sanity. I gave up on rational thought after a while and just related the play-by-play while Taylor listened.

"The rats are swarming. Pigeons and those skinny birds with brownish feathers and sharp black beaks keep flapping in through the open window, landing on these new bodies and taking what they want. There aren't any sparrows. The birds are fighting the rats over the fleshy bits."

I couldn't tell Taylor everything. My mouth wouldn't form the words, the fact that police uniforms covered the arms and torsos of the corpses, but nothing protected their faces. I was sobbing. At this point my battery was dying and I was too afraid to go into the dark bedroom where my charger was plugged into the wall, and too upset to hang up the phone and call 911 again. Some superstitious thought from my reptilian brain insisted that if I stopped watching for even a second, the vermin would discover me too, or the flash of darkness would somehow cross the airshaft. I felt that I had been designated the guardian of this profane space. I took my assignment seriously, far more seriously than Taylor did. As I reported the ghastly goings-on, Taylor kept asking me to meet up somewhere, the Chinese place on the corner or Afghan Kabob Hut, or some other ethnic restaurant with huge portions and small price tags, where we could feed the fear and laugh away the afterimages, send them to that place New Yorkers send ghastly memories of glimpsed horrors. I said no, and finally extended an invitation. "Come over, let yourself in, keep me company."

"I don't know."

"Please," I said. "I don't want to be alone."

My phone battery died, cutting off any response. I knelt before my window, my face leaning into the still air, wishing for a breeze. I thought I could smell the rot in the air, but that could have been the usual stench of the city. I didn't know what I was waiting for. I only knew I had to wait.

But funny thing, death. Especially your own. It is very disorienting.

Taylor never showed up to discover my body, so I wandered the neighborhood, drifting from the kerosene smells of the halal carts to the sweet cool breezes emanating from high-end soap boutiques. Sometimes I would be trapped for a while in an air-conditioned shop that drew me in with aromas of lavender or patchouli, cinnamon orange, or lemon mint. After death, I seemed inexorably drawn to aromas, and not just the nice ones: the thundercloud of a diesel engine, the warm oily vents in low-end deli storefronts, the various dogs and their sweaty owners, the poisonous yet alluring smells from dry cleaners, even the impossible reek of hot restaurant compost left on the curb in leaking plastic bags. I was completely unable to find Taylor's place though I'd been there a thousand times. And then I couldn't find my way back home, either. New York has too many smells, I've been absorbed into the maze of them. I have been wandering for days, perhaps weeks.

I wonder whatever became of my neighbor's apartment. Or mine. I wonder if it was a summoned darkness that killed us. I wonder at the irony that with such dark evil within reach, my neighbor still lived in that shithole apartment, seduced strangers, and was the typical underachieving, lonely, ordinary human being that the City minted by the thousand.

Funny. People never visit that area. The strange experimental restaurants and bizarre small shops in the unnamed neighborhood between Chinatown and the East River are just slightly out of comfortable walking distance;

there are no subway stations, not even any bus stops on our street. There are no shops, no popup art galleries with cats and coffee and artisanal cocktails. The tenements are full of squatters, junkies, and meth heads, and no sane person wants to co-habit that level of desperation. Could be our two buildings are roped off with police tape. Could be the area is empty. People walk past blocks like that in New York City every day—a row of empty townhouses, walled off with construction plywood, and you think to yourself, *Huh, development, what a shame, those old walls are probably full of stories.*

The Mayor of Flashback

Svetlana Grimskaya. For twenty years he had assumed her name was an alias. Twenty! Can it have been that long? The Russian barfly had whispered her name across his throat, back in the dank St. Petersburg hole where he had found her lurking like a viper, glittery and lethal. He believed it was a lie, a slippery dream invented to separate stupid Americans from their wallets.

Turns out, nope, that's her actual name. Go figure. And she has to be in her forties now. Or at least thirty-eight.

She asks to friend him on Facebook, and a memory like the woozy bitterness of absinthe scrapes across Jim's hard-won happiness. Svetlana Grimskaya is a buried past life—American Jim lost to Russia, a young, proud MBA student staggering to keep upright in a cage of velvet walls hung with taxidermy. The underground bar could not have been more stereotypical. Tsars would have laughed into their sleeves to see how wide his eyes grew as he followed the clatter of his grad-school friends down the stone steps. Their faces glowed with naiveté born of extreme self-confidence—the arrogance that announced them as perfect victims to all but other Americans.

Without leaving his luxury apartment at the South Street Seaport—even this is a measure of his success: the loft had tripled in value since the school had opened across Peck Slip, the run-down New York City neighborhood redeemed and labeled historic, its citizens newly wealthy—Jim leans back in his ergonomic desk chair until the black leather groans and he travels to January, 1999.

A trio of tarnished, low-hanging chandeliers set to their dimmest glow allowed the yellowed teeth of a stuffed bear to glint in fierce final pretense. Svetlana lounged against a furry elk, calling to mind every vodka ad Young American Jim had ever taped to a dorm room ceiling.

A vibrant licorice scent sailed arrow-like through air dense with other smells; even Svetlana's tar-thick cloud of cigarette smoke was pierced. He was suffocating, unable to breathe. Was it the surreal situation or this super-blonde's too-direct gaze? His twenty-six years had diminished in comparison to the age of the underground bar, the age of this Russian city's foundations (replete with echoes of a tour guide reciting numbers of the dead beneath the streets, if those echoes held any truth then this bar was surely surrounded by skeletons), the jaded look in Svetlana's eye, daring his American voice to mention death or sadness and not sound trite.

A buff Estonian waiter lit the liqueur on fire, inverted the brandy glass on paper, warmed sugar with a spoon. Jim gazed at the liquid green whirlpool in its fragile glass globe. Thought of an alien apocalypse. Verdant flames, dancing on a syrupy sea.

Absinthe!

She was laughing at his shock; he was paying. She staggered against him…

The images jumble and include sheaves of blonde hair sweeping across his stubbled chin and bare shoulders, and fingers exploring the musty corners of his unwashed body, which embarrassed him now, and certainly all must have happened much later in the night if they'd happened at all. Names were brushed lightly on bare skin: his, hers, mingling with lies in a cocktail of international accents.

Jim tastes the anise of those memories through the layers of his current very-adult life each time he checks Svetlana's Facebook status, which happens two or three times a day, for weeks. In February, Svetlana posts she is in town for a six-month rotation at her investment firm. He never calls, does not message directly, he only "likes" every Facebook status and discovers she finds the outmoded Foursquare app scintillating. This amuses him the same way it had bemused him when she'd been intrigued by the handful of tech toys he'd brought to Russia. To him they were passé, to her a window. He immediately downloads the ridiculous app and then haunts her check-ins through late winter, early Spring, and into summer:

at a Meatpacking District restaurant
in Macy's
at Lincoln Center

in Central Park

at work, always at work.

She is often the Foursquare "mayor" of her office, even though she is still only a junior analyst. He tries not to think of how old she must be, tries not to wonder why she hasn't truly made it in the world. He is embarrassed by his own wealth, his multi-million-dollar home. His wife and child. His credit card debt and mortgage and his indifference to it all. Seeing her pop up like that on social media, memories naturally follow. Then fantasies.

The dream of Svetlana soon overpowers the reality. Specter-like, he flutters through her virtual day, imbuing each location with assignations, repetitions, conversations, and above all with sex.

It is after Kiki's bedtime when he sees Svetlana has checked-in at the Seaport. She is within walking distance, and the stomach drops out of his games. As if fate has orchestrated reality to harm him, he and his wife are not semi-intertwined on the sofa in the middle of their usual Netflix binge—tonight, of all nights, Rose wanted to finish reading her novel, leaving him at odds. Bored.

Like in Russia: It's destiny. He spots the check-in and then there's a few words, a quick peck on the cheek, and an airy, wifely: "Of course. Say hi to your friend for me. I'm fine; I have a book."

Just like he's always imagined.

***

They are having a beer in his local Irish pub and they sit like a dating couple just below the windows of his apartment. Her mouth whispers his name as if it is pronounced with multiple consonants and strange Eastern European vowels. *Džym.* In her accent, his name is a luxury item. A taste of caviar on the tip of her tongue, salty, fishy, unobtainable, hypersexual.

"Svetlana," he replies as if to blot out the fantasy, as if her real name attached to a real human will remind him that these particular cobblestone streets belong to old New York, not to czarist Russia. And then he mentions his wife and his daughter. His wife. His wife again. Rose. Kiki. Rose. Rose. He speaks their names again and again, like a fatal cancer he can't stop describing.

"After the playdate, Kiki stopped to smell the tulips."

Why is he telling awkward stories of Manhattan in April? It is midsummer. The breeze off the East River is too brief and halfhearted to affect the heavy and hot air. Like in a Russian bathhouse when someone opens the door, then reconsiders. Svetlana's nose wrinkles but her forehead remains utterly smooth.

"I was surprised to see tulips here," she says. "They—decorate? Is this the word?—every sidewalk in Manhattan. Springtime here was like Holland. I was in Holland when you posted the thing about your nine-eleven experience. Too terrible."

This was not a conversation he wanted. He never wanted to talk about 9/11 again. It had happened so long ago, he usually could avoid the subject with locals. He stayed in on the anniversary, hid out with his wife, watching Netflix. There was a beautiful new mall there, now. Gorgeous fountains. A park with rows and rows of trees. Kiki's preschool was on the far side of the site. He always took the long way around. He was on the verge of revealing this, his darkest secret, to her. Would a Russian understand this impossible attachment to history, the fact that he had never gotten over that day? That because of that day, he still feels mistrust in his bones—not of Arabs but of humanity in general? Would she recognize the underlying fear that at any moment life could be stolen from you? Or would she laugh at him?

Her eyes lit up: "Oh! Did you ever make it to Amsterdam? Remember how we dreamed of it? That Museum of Sex we were so excited to see? It was just a boring tourist trap. Imagine? Very, very stupid."

"Tulips have a bad smell. Kiki was so disappointed that something so lovely would smell so bad."

Again, her nose wrinkled and there was a slight pause. "She should try corpse flower."

Now the pause was his. "Is that real?"

"In Borneo. It can make you sick. Remember when we talked about running to Borneo? I went for vacation one time. Nice beaches. Such good fruits. And lots of crazy monkeys. Shit-crazy monkeys. I couldn't believe."

Her long legs cross and uncross and he watches through the glass tabletop as if it were porn.

"Isn't this view so gorgeous?" she finally coos into the awkward silence. "I'm so happy you wanted to meet."

She tries too hard. It makes him stammer. There is too much effort at this table. His unfinished craft beer sweats onto the coaster. She should be done with him; he's a married man. She should stalk off. Then he could follow her, grab her arm, twist her around. Steal a kiss.

His wife is reading that sort of novel upstairs while his daughter sleeps.

"Three bedrooms," he tells Svetlana, "bought in anticipation of two kids, only the second child never happened. We only have Kiki. Even she was a little hard to come by."

Over low brownstones that used to house bordellos for lonely sailors, the Brooklyn Bridge twinkles against the summer night sky: She is right, the view is lovely. Over the last few years, he has stopped noticing. Outdoor seating. History. Possibilities. His head swims with looking up. He focuses these days on sidewalks: steering his three-year old past broken glass and the all-too-frequent landmines that local dogs leave. He has become a guide to playgrounds and swimming pools. He used to know where absinthe was served in St. Petersburg. Now he knows where public bathrooms can be found on the way to Montessori.

"We're toilet training Kiki for the second time. Her old preschool used to put her in Pull-ups for their daily walk—it undid all Rose's work. We changed schools. They're teaching her French."

The table shakes with—*What was that?* Gunshots? Earthquake? Explosions? Loud popping sounds jostle his ribs and echo off the flat spines of the nearby skyscrapers. He is suffocating. His breath catches in his throat. The reaction is physical. His chest tightens as if he is again buried in the dust, running for his life, not knowing what wall will crumble. The air is thick. Too thick. He forces the air into his lungs, feeling like something has him by the ankle and is dragging him down, down, down. Back to the place where he left his sense of safety. Back to the moment his arrogance died. Back to the few ugly days of history that lodged themselves between his DNA and ribosomes and forced him to relive his helplessness and acknowledge his mortality whenever there is an explosion, however harmless.

She has gone silent. Watching him. Interest has wrinkled the corners of her eyes and the smoothly Botoxed skin in the center of her forehead; it has puckered her ruby lips into a sphincter. She looks forty. Forty-five. Older.

He tells himself that he is safe. Safe! It's not a terrorist bomb. Construction. Just construction. Lower Manhattan is always under construction. He works his jaw while Svetlana looks at him with the expression of a cat glimpsing the tip of a mouse's tail. Another pop: They look up at the dark sky in tandem. The skyscrapers surrounding them light up in a pale blue, then a red. Not construction explosives. Fireworks. Just fireworks.

They echo off the facing buildings, sounding like ordinance. He can smell sulfur on the breeze. His intestines go soft, and he feels compelled to get to his feet to check and make sure that they really are fireworks. (They are, he knows.)

She follows him, wordless.

Beautiful, sexy Svetlana has come to the Seaport for the

annual jazz festival. The weekend of music is ending now in the way of all American traditions: with noises and lights that simulate the beautiful side of violence. Fireworks, meant to impress. He makes himself breathe more slowly; embarrassed to be so terribly upset by an ordinary if sudden sound. She pretends she doesn't notice, and he is grateful to her. The twirl and hoot of distant saxophones remind him that he has pulled her away from a party. Across the large cobblestone plaza, the swanky Italian restaurant is lit in splashes of blue and green and gold. Young couples gripped in romantic passion disentangle to pull out cellphones and document the unexpected shower of lights. After each burst the couples kiss, as if playing out choreography.

Meanwhile, he'd nearly ducked under his table thinking he was in danger. Bombs. Explosives. He'd even thought God might be striking him down.

PTSD of the civilian. Brief. Stupid. The sort that is too embarrassing to medicate or explore in therapy. The sort you live with and laugh off as best you can.

From the shadow of the pub's awning, Jim can't see the sky blossoms, just a corona of purple light. He wipes sweat from his forehead, his temples; winces at the next loud bang and almost walks off alone, but reaches back to take Svetlana's hand. She accepts. The contact is time travel, and takes him to Russia, years before terrorism hit home.

January 1999: the explosions are centered in his groin, his heart, his soul. Her hair sweeps his chest, his stomach. Vibrant green liquid swirls in a lost bowl of glass. The sulfur stinks of licorice and sex.

Svetlana says he looks pale; asks if the fireworks have frightened him. He laughs it off in his practiced way.

He was right there when the towers fell, he admits to her. Covered in acrid dust.

He stops talking and remembers.

Eating it. Too numb to weep. First, keeping his clothes in bags for evidence, then throwing them down the compactor after the EPA told them to get rid of the couch and equally contaminated rug. Down the chute. Incinerated. Lost.

He regrets it, even now. What if that dust could have helped someone? Proved something? People are dying of cancer and no one believes they got it from inhaling pulverized fuselage decades ago. Rose's brother has been embroiled in a lawsuit since 2005. Jim could have kept a souvenir. One jar of the ghastly gray powder. It could be saving lives. What does he have instead? A huge pencil with Novgorod etched in its side in Cyrillic. (He does not remember Novgorod, though he remembers the vendor with his dwarflike beard, who insisted on carving the word with a hunter's knife while Jim watched.) He also has a pile of sugar packets from various Russian palaces. He has an ashtray lined in amber. He doesn't even smoke. These things gather dust of the ordinary kind in his office, where he rarely works, preferring to work from home, to be near Kiki and Rose.

A bloom of colors explodes across the night sky and his arm is around Svetlana's waist.

She giggles and he knows he should put his arm down. He does not.

"Really, I had such a great time at the Met, today; I managed to see the whole thing," she is saying and he is biting his tongue, telling himself it doesn't matter that she is wrong. She can't possibly have seen the whole museum.

Let it go.

Twenty years ago, she had mocked him for seeing the Hermitage in one day.

The fireworks pop in red and silver.

He never lets anything go. He still harbors anger at her for Russia—her soft hair falls over his shoulder as she rests her head against him to better see the sky change colors—anger for the way she never made eye contact while dancing. She was twenty then, or said she was, and her miniskirt might have been the height of Petersburg fashion, but to him and his grad-school buddies, it was little more than a flag of surrender.

She had mocked him then too, laughing that he was so jealous, an old man already, this American who had showed up in her country and, after sleeping with her once, treated her like a wife. *I'm no one's wife*, she had bellowed to the crowded bar. The students drank their shots. The women continued their flatteries. In Russia, the dance music is so loud, no one can hear you scream.

"I'm so glad we found each other again," she whispers. Her breath tickles his neck. His body corrects and, as if she were made of supple clay, they fit together better.

He glances up at his living room windows. Rose would have also heard the fireworks. She had also lived through the towers; loud sounds in tight quarters can make her cry. Her brother, the fireman that lived. Together she and Jim carry the ghosts of friends in their sudden flare-ups of anger, the ghosts of strangers in their groundless fears; ghosts upon ghosts swim in every tear that falls when they are happy. (Crying when happy was a disease they had all caught that awful day; they had lost the ability to trust a smile.) Jim's living room blinds are, as usual, half-closed against the amber streetlights, and he can't tell if they are angled up, which is safe, or angled down, which means Rose can spy. Could right now be watching. Is that movement?

His phone rings and he leaps away from Svetlana as if she has caught fire. He brings the phone from his pocket and he looks up at the window again.

"What's up, honey?"

"Sorry to bug you. Are you having fun?"

"Yes." He thinks it will seem less guilty to be honest. "Why are you calling? Is everything okay? Is Kiki okay?"

He hears in Rose's easy laugh that she's nowhere near the window; hasn't been all night. "Kiki's fine. We're just out of milk, and I wanted to know if you could run down to the Duane Reade and grab a gallon."

"Sure. Later."

"It's open 24 hours."

"I know."

"Organic. 2%."

"I know."

Now he hears her pause. Sees the blinds open. He waves, glad that Svetlana has taken a few steps to check her own e-mail on her own smartphone, so Rose won't have to see how well a

Russian girl can preserve her looks.

Svetlana's sleeves are long and translucent, but from a distance the fabric seems opaque, and her tight skirt does not ride up the way it did when she was seated. The Russian way: publicly demure, privately audacious.

"We were looking at the fireworks, did they bother you?" He says this to erase the knowledge of Svetlana's deep cleavage, the gold clasp on the front of her bra, so inviting.

"I was reading. Is that her?"

Svetlana follows her texting thumbs across the plaza and back to the pub looking for better signal. Like all girls from northern European cities, she is an expert at walking cobblestones in stilettos. He gets a Facebook e-mail notification that she has checked in at his bar, with him. It is disconcerting to still have Rose on the phone when this happens.

"That's her. Milk. Anything else?"

"No. She's pretty."

"Yes. She's Russian."

"I was picturing a cleaning woman; you know, the fat dumpy kind."

"Oh. She's not like that."

"Clearly."

In the pause, fireworks explode into cascading waterfalls of blue and white. The white particles hover and shimmer until they wink out. Svetlana beckons from the shade of the pub's awning where she has seated herself again.

"Well. I better get back. I don't want to be out all night. I'll get the milk. Kiki's okay?"

"She's fine. I told you. Have fun."

"Bye." He waves at her and she waves back and closes the shades all the way. Her trust lands heavy, like the final curtain of a tragic opera. She trusts him too much.

Svetlana's skirt has ridden up. Her thighs are smooth and perfect. The streetlights paint them rosy amber. The fireworks sound like gunshots. Echoes that careen off skyscrapers. A rain of unexpected artillery. It is horrific.

"May I smoke?"

He smiles at her question, nods. Smoking feels quaint to him, a thing you do in college, a thing you eventually outgrow. It always surprises him when someone his age hasn't yet quit. In Russia, Svetlana had blown the smoke directly into his face, to see if he would turn away. He watches her light up.

She exhales to her left, over her shoulder, as if whispering an aside to someone invisible. Through his sadness, he can't bring himself to take up her free hand, though she has left it on the table: a treat between beers.

"I have an early day tomorrow," he tells her. "Kiki gets up at 5:30."

"That's very early."

"Since she was a baby. We can't cure her."

Svetlana nods. Blows smoke at the ghost behind her. "I wanted to have baby. Had a boyfriend, but he was so stupid. An Italian, stupid and pretty. I got pregnant and he got another girlfriend. So I got abortion. I am not sorry, but also, yes. Some days, yes."

"I love my daughter."

"I can see that." A wicked smile. "Are you going to let her go to Russia when she gets grown?"

The image of a grown Kiki, that name on a lanky girl of eighteen or twenty. She will already have a tattoo, kept secret from her mother. Some other things she will keep: her curly brown hair, his eyes, her eagerness to try anything new. What else? Her love of sweets, of adventure, of dance, of music. Her tendency to fight the rules, her curiosity of all things bad. But she will also acquire breasts and legs and a fashion sense and a cellphone. And she will fall in love.

He is going to lose his daughter. She is going to grow up and become something else he wasn't able to save.

His body feels pummeled. He struggles to keep his chin from quivering. Presses his fingers against his lips as if he is trying to suppress a little laugh.

"Of course." He shrugs. "Why not. Traveling was a great experience. I don't regret a minute of it."

January 1999: holding Svetlana's hair back so she could puke into what passed for a toilet in the absinthe bar. Vomit splashing his feet, causing them both to stumble against the shit-smeared wall. Grabbing her arms so they didn't both fall.

Fucking against the sink. Next night, returning for more, though not quite so much, and the fucking happened in a bed. She had learned something. Had found a limit. He had done the opposite. They traded names. He had assumed hers was invented on the spot.

Svetlana Grimskaya. An impossible name.

"I'm here for the rest of July and half of August," she says.

"Four weeks." It is an offer. Embarrassment hangs between them like underpants left to dry on a shower rod.

"Let me get this," he replies, laying a platinum credit card over the check. Kiki, smelling the tulips, got furious that the different colors didn't have different scents. She'd wanted flowers to have flavors, like lollipops. Reality had betrayed her. He signs for the beers, speaks his intention to buy milk on the way home. Svetlana offers to walk him to the store.

He nods once, as if the smallest movement on his part might sway his resolve.

They walk together the four blocks to the all-night drugstore, and to his surprise she enters the brightly lit space with him. He searches her face in the hard, fluorescent lighting, but despite the faint brushstrokes around her eyes suggesting lines that might become permanent in the next ten years, she is no less desirable. If anything, her eyes are brighter and her smile more open. If only time had aged her faster than him.

Crowds spill down Fulton Street away from the Seaport. Everyone is drunk, staggering and laughing and waving bright cellphones and leaning on each other to take selfies, their arms embracing the air in a false hug. It is a river that Svetlana wishes to rejoin. He says something boring and forgettable.

Let's do this again. Or possibly, *It was great seeing you.* He wants to clutch her to him, even here, at the head of the snack aisle, but instead his lips brush across her forehead in the dry, fatherly way he has honed with Kiki.

He watches the glass doors slide open to accept his offering. Watches how she adjusts her skirt. Watches her golden hair vanish into the tide of humanity.

Returns to reality where he must buy the milk.

The line is long and the cashier is sluggish, so he pulls up the Foursquare app on his phone and checks in at the drugstore. A message announces that as the mayor of Duane Reade he gets a 10% discount.

Rose texts: *Also decongestant. 24-hour. Ask at counter.*

He texts back: *I'm the mayor of Duane Reade.*

His wife texts him a smiley face, the cashier calls next, and Jim is doing as well as anyone.

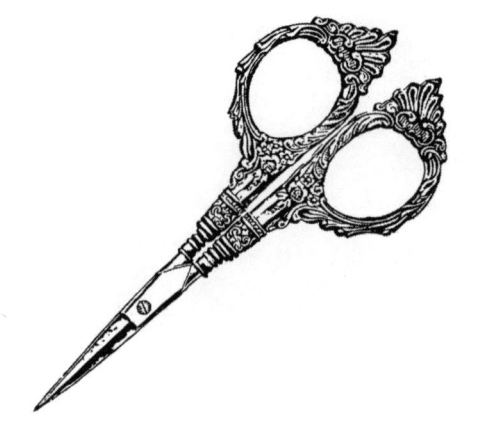

The Scissors of Hope & Despair

Granny's old-world Kazakh accent thickened as her mind unraveled. She landed in Baltimore in early childhood and lived nearly a century in this country among other émigré Kazakhs, harming her own people and harboring grudges. Her brutal life story was a source of pride in my family—had been a source of pride, that is, while the family was still around. I am the only one left to visit. It's a chore. Family is often a chore.

Mufti Isham tells me it is my beautiful responsibility, not a chore.

I wish I could ask my parents what they think about it.

"We play game in minute," Granny says, struggling to her feet, "I'm off for second cup tea. Salima, want?"

I dislike Granny's bitter herbals. What started as a delightful floral tisane of jasmine would soon have a few drops of thyme oil for beauty, a sprig of a passionflower for kindness, and far too much anise. I want a scotch. "No thank you, Granny."

The door to the kitchen swings shut, leaving only the antique peppery scent of the old woman, masked by the ever-present bowls of lavender-water. Late afternoon sunlight filters through the white curtains and illuminates the panic button, the only indication that the apartment is part of a retirement community. The sunlight also enhances the layer of gray dust on every surface. I suppress an urge to pick up Granny's lace doilies and shake them out. The sunbeams are already alive with dust. The room looks like a still from a B-grade horror movie, the definition of "seemingly normal." Any time I spend in this facility seems slow, as if each minute is as burdened as I am by the knowledge that Granny is succumbing to senility.

Out of irrepressible habit, I inspect my phone. It never works at Granny's, and today is no different. It won't even tell the time. Something about Granny's magic messes with technology.

I have been coming every Tuesday night. Two long years of staring at this chessboard, losing game after game, wondering as I move the ancient pieces if it is true: This chess set holds the last of my family. I can't push her. I can only wait. She called me by my mother's name, Umit, twice this afternoon, and looked dazed when I asked to play our usual game of chess.

"Oh. Do I still know how?" she had asked, much in the tone of someone instructed to juggle three balls after years in a colorless office job.

"In fact, you always beat me," I'd replied. And this had brought Granny to pull the small brass key from her pocket and unlock the arcane cabinet where she kept the chessboard. Never once has this woman been able to eschew a possible victory.

And now?

I am finally alone with both the board and Granny's sewing basket. If Mufti Isham is not completely off his rocker, if all this madness is not just the fanciful storytelling of old people, I might be able to bring my family back. All of them. I find it impossible to believe, even though it is my only hope of ever seeing them again.

"Don't touch anything!" Granny's voice pierces the thick kitchen door, travels the dust as if summoned.

My hand hovers in the air above the basket. "I didn't!" I shout back.

"Mint tea?" my grandmother calls, forgetting that I don't want any.

"No, but thank you for offering," I reply.

I remember how my father always smelled of mint and pipe smoke, because he hid in the garden to smoke and would chew the mint in an unsuccessful attempt to hide the smoking from my mother. As a little kid I thought it was hilarious that both he and my mother perpetuated the lie, each fully aware of what the other was doing. At bedtime one night while she was reading me a translated Kazakh folk tale, I asked her about this deception, and instead of brushing my question away, she lowered the book and told me that sometimes, to save someone's dignity, falsehoods had to be perpetuated. Dignity was important, she had said, then fell to sucking on the earpiece of her reading glasses until, tired of the silence, I demanded to know why. She nodded as if making a bargain with herself. Then she told me this truth: The appearance of civility is what keeps society in order.

This is why I perpetuate the lie that my grandmother is independent. I feel uncomfortable about that, but it doesn't stop me from visiting. Granny always wins at chess, but I always agree to play another round. It makes me feel closer to my family.

Over the last month, a second sadness has been growing unmentioned (like a sorrowful Spanish moss) over our weekly games as I watch Granny's wickedness fade. Nowadays the old dear generally thinks she's just another normal senior citizen. More often than not, she watches cooking shows and grouses at the evening news instead of casting spells to ruin skin or cause hearing loss. The nurses that come by every morning and leave at noon all think that Granny is the sweetest thing in the world. Sure—when she isn't ending lives, prolonging pain, and entrapping people within inanimate objects.

To try to get my pulse back to normal, I fiddle with my phone again. Nothing. Random letters appear and move around on the screen as if trying to tell me something, but I can't make heads or tails of the message. I tuck the useless technology into my backpack and look hard again at the chess set on the low coffee table. Granny frequently reminds me she brought it over from the old country at great personal peril. She has also said the board is now populated by my mother, my father, and Granny's myriad brothers and cousins and uncles and aunts. And others. People I don't know. I lift a pawn and scrutinize it, but all pawns look the same. White and red bone. It could be my baby brother, it could be the dog, it could be that horrible uncle who cut our lawn and who wouldn't stop whistling at me whenever I went to my car. He was awful. I'd sacrifice him without remorse, if only I knew which piece he was.

"You sure I can't fix some tea? Perhaps a bite to eat?" Granny calls. The squeal of the kettle makes me wince. One of the pawns trembles. Ah. So that's the dog. I make mental note of it.

"I'm fine, Granny. Thank you."

It dawns on me that the whistle also means the tea will be served soon.

"Actually, Granny? If you have a little milk? I'd love a bit of warm milk and honey. And maybe a cookie?"

Clattering, rattling teacups. It's now or never.

I dig a hand deep into the sewing basket, assured of at least a few more seconds of privacy. My fingers nudge past hard spools of thread, lace trim, and many, many thimbles, some of which seemed designed to entrap exploring fingers. Keeping my eyes fixed on the kitchen door, I allow my fingertips to dance across the prick of needles, tumble through the seabed of lost buttons—there! The velvet parcel! My fingers sink softly around the promise it holds. The packet twitches, startling me a little. The gold-tipped scissors are in there, wrapped up tight. A whisper of melody thrums from inside the wrapping, like bells played with feathers. Beyond the kitchen door, Granny's voice hums in perfect harmony.

I assure myself that it's probably just coincidence.

Granny's things from the old country often seem attuned to her physical being even when they are not proximal to her. It's the ancient way. When I turned eighteen, I had only just started to notice glimmers of the family gift, when Granny began showing real signs of senility. Losing recipes and keys was one thing, but the paranoid fits—! I couldn't trust her to teach me without turning against me as she had with the rest of the family. I'd sworn off the old ways entirely after moving away; my mother assured Granny I was subsumed in my education and too busy to visit. This pacified her for a time, because she'd liked the idea that I was using my brain.

On my part, I made diminishing efforts to visit and frequently skipped family events, so I wasn't surprised when no one showed up for my college graduation. I wrote them off, feeling justified and valiant in surrounding myself with educated friends instead. But several months after the last time I ever spoke with my mother, Mufti Isham called out of nowhere and begged me to attend to the responsibilities of my swiftly deteriorating Granny. There wasn't anybody else, he'd explained; it had to be a blood relative. He convinced me to rekindle my relationship with my grandmother, told me about the scissors. He'd explained to my flat disbelief that I had to bring them all back before she smashed the whole set.

In typical ornery fashion, Granny demanded that I play chess with her.

She could be vicious that way.

I pick up the bishop, search the empty frown across his face for some sign of familiarity, some feeling that this is Uncle Mac or Aunt Mel, maybe his mischievous eye twinkle, or something to indicate her love of melodrama, but of course nothing stands out. Not even a glimmer of warmth to show that a living being is trapped inside the bone. I rub the nub that makes the bishop's hat. Thirty-two people ticked off Granny in her life. Enough to make a perfect set. I examine each piece for my baby brother's jolly smile, a sign of his kindness, his sweet, simple wisdom, any hint of his ability to accept chaos as a meaningful part of life.

He's the one I miss the most.

Over the past two years, as Granny's mind softened, she had started to speak without caution. She told stories of how powerful it made her feel to restore a broken marriage, and how lovely it was to sweep the clouds from a graduation day, a pimple from a bride's forehead, or leukemia from a beloved cat. Listening to her ramble, I had started to wonder whether magic was less of a family curse and more of a family tradition—like cooking, something you didn't appreciate when forced to learn it, but if you had approached it at whim and for no personal gain, you could become devoted. When Granny boasted she had been the cause of the sudden rainstorm that had saved me from a probable mugging when I was secretly visiting a boyfriend in DC, I had to believe her. I had never shared that story with anyone. Maybe, as Mufti Isham insisted, Granny did own a pair of magic scissors with the ability to bring back the past.

It is true that my family vanished more than two years ago. Perhaps they just packed up and returned to the old country, leaving me behind. It is possible. The political climate—as it was. People did run. The schoolteacher. The librarian. But my family loved this country; they had dug in, had bought a business, grown roots. A Kazakh neighbor insisted demons carried them off. My liberal college friends blamed the government. ICE.

Deportations. They offered legal help, advice, the websites of fringe groups questioning the disappearances of dissidents.

When it seemed that my family might not be alone, I felt comforted and hopeful. It seemed less like magic and more like politics.

Still. There were no paper trails. No witnesses. I spent a frantic year searching. All the while, Granny maintained that she had trapped them in the chess set with the others.

Mufti Isham said the same.

Ultimately, I've started to believe them both. Because that way, I could believe I might possibly get my family back. It would be nice to show my father my diploma. I would like to hug my mother again, to stay up all night eating ice cream out of a carton with my baby brother. I need them. At least I know about the scissors, and it is only a matter of getting to them when Granny isn't looking.

You'd think, in a year, I might have managed—but Granny is a sharp old thing, as nutty as she is, and she senses things. Playing chess reminds her to protect the pieces, to guard the sewing basket. Her nurses say she's crazy, the way she carries it everywhere.

If only the scissors could really bring them all back. I untie the silky blue ribbon, and it slips away from the velvet like a dream at daybreak, vanishing before it touches the wooden floor. The scissors are prettier than I remember, and their melody is soft and haunting. Shaped like a pair of herons with emerald eyes, their pointed beaks kiss the sky, the bright blades gleaming as though recently sharpened.

One bird is named Hope. The other Despair. I do not know which is which, nor how to tell them apart. They always appeared together in the old books, and Granny said they always arrive together in life as well. To separate them is to create havoc.

Each individual feather caresses my fingers with real warmth. It is not me who is petting the birds, it is the scissors competing for my affection like a pair of puppies wanting their heads scratched.

"It's too quiet. Are you in my basket?" Granny calls from the kitchen.

I look down. "No, Granny. I'm not!"

"Stay out," Granny says. "Some things there, you will not predict."

I hold the scissors high and snip the air. An old man shuffles into the room.

My breath catches. Is this Grandfather? It looks just like him. Sixteen years have passed since I've seen him. Was his face always so gray, his chin this bristly, his nose this leaky? His watery eyes look at me without recognition. Grampa settles into the leather recliner near the bookshelves and puts his feet up. He does not speak to me, does not react to me at all. He stares at his feet, as if lost in memory.

A moment passes while I stare at him. He digs a finger around in his ear like he used to at the dinner table, causing all the women to groan and the men to laugh. No one is here to react but me. I do not know what this means. Is he real? What will Gran say when she sees him? Will she be able to see him at all? Will she trap me in the chess piece in his place? I drop the scissors in the basket, not bothering with the velvet bag, then hold one hand with the other to stop the trembling.

"I just took your queen," I call to the kitchen, making the move after I speak. The board had shuffled itself—Granny would never have left herself open like this. I feel the winning streak coming on, but I don't feel proud. I feel like I cheated. "*En garde*."

"Leave scissor, girl. You are too young for understand things."

"I'm twenty-four, Gran," I retort. "An adult. Who do you think pays for all this?"

Granny's sigh blows through the apartment in wisps of purple and gold. Dust is disturbed from the knickknacks, from the books, from the tablecloths and curtains. The multicolored sigh curls around Granny's old husband, enveloping him in magic while the dust in the air swirls thick. I sneeze. When my eyes reopen, the old man has frozen in an attitude of expectation. He doesn't appear to breathe; he's just waiting.

The bone queen has not budged. The rook with which I'd threatened her is missing. I search the floor, but it has vanished.

Granny's slippers hush closer. "I'm not crazy, girl. I have my whole mind."

"No one said you were crazy, Granny."

"I can see it. I can see how you look, like I don't know you hate my good teas. I see you question my judgment, question my mind. You think I old lady, with blind eyes?"

I press my lips together, considering. I recall the vapid blue of Granny's eyes as they accepted the ugly accusations of the day-nurse. The sigh of pleasure as the condescending Ecuadoran doctor urged her to up her dose of Mobic; he'd be happy to prescribe more, because what did it really matter at her age? The unchecked line of drool from Granny's lips as the handsome Dominican night-nurse gently groomed and called her guapa, even as the brush in his hand clumped thick with her white hairs. No, Granny is not herself. She was wicked once—evil, even. Now she is soft. I search for the missing rook.

"He was bad man," Granny clucks as she sets down her tray of cookies and tea. "Your grandfather. I was wicked, but he? Was cruel. I took revenge, only. He hurt people. No reason. Me, he liked to make suffer. He deserved… " Her voice trails as she takes in the new state of the board, the scissors, the guilt heating my cheeks. The old man remains seated in the corner, immobile. She does not look his way. I'm dying to ask her if she sees him, but I'm afraid of either answer.

Granny lowers herself into her chair. I wring my hands. I know the look in her eyes.

"The rook." Her words are little more than puff in the air. Her gnarled hand digs between the cushions of the sofa. Her husband stands and leaves the room. She fishes out the rook, returns it to the side of the chessboard. "Salima. You can take over whole board. You know enough. But you have no strategy. No young persons do. Young persons are thinking of winning only. Is not enough." Her fingertips caress the air and for a split second, I feel the agony of all the imprisoned souls on the board. When the air stills, the feeling ebbs away. It's like being grabbed in a dreadful, crushing hug and then released. I gasp for air.

"Winning. Losing. No real meaning," Granny mutters.

I scowl. Of course winning has meaning. The whole point of chess is to win. I think longingly of that scotch again. Or at least a glass of wine. Anything to ease the thrumming that has begun in my head, which always begins after staying too long with Granny.

"You're just saying that," I tell her.

"Take that warm milk, dear," she says. "Still hot." Yet a stronger heat rises in my neck. She is so dismissive. Always so dismissive.

"I don't think I will, thanks," I reply. "Also, I should let you know that I'm not sure I'll be visiting as often in the coming months. It's coming up on Fall. I'll be busy with grad school."

Granny looks sadly over the chessboard. "But middle of game."

I decide to throw caution to the wind. "You should let them all go, Gran."

"Young persons. So rash. If you knew everything, you'd know why they must stay."

I can't believe it. This is almost an admission. I push forward, on the attack. "Granny, tell me or don't tell me. You always toy with me like this. I'm tired of it. I'm twenty-four years old. I have a master's degree in comparative religion. I start classes for my Ph.D. in September. I'm not a child."

Granny slurps her tea. White mist steams up her little round glasses. "That study you take. It is—what is word? Goofy."

I pick up the rook. I put it down. Pick it up again.

"Then tell me just one of them, Gran. Tell me this one."

"That one. Rook."

"This one story, Granny, and I'll leave you alone."

Granny removes her glasses and wipes the lenses in careful triangles, almost as if she is drawing a ward.

"No," she finally says. "No, I don't think I will."

I rise to go. "I'm done."

"I tell you *your* story instead."

"Oh." The sound escapes my lips entirely by accident. I want to punish her for treating me with such condescension, but I can't help it. I'm curious. Is Granny going to tell me that I used to be a doll, or a mouse, or a toy piano once upon a time? Will she explain why my family was never emotionally present, even before they were trapped in the chess set? I am ten, and no one cares if my homework is done. I am thirteen, and no one asks if I got home safely from the party. I am sixteen, and no one notices my brief pregnancy, either before or after. I am twenty, and they all ignore my well-paying but demeaning "modeling" career—at least the photographers never show my face; sometimes that seems like a blessing, sometimes it makes me think my face wasn't even pretty enough for *that*. Then, I am suddenly twenty-two and everyone vanishes, leaving me behind with Granny.

She stares at me, waiting. I sink back onto the sofa cushions, cowed by possibilities. What is "my story," exactly? Do I even have one?

"Okay," I whisper.

Granny's head tilts as if appraising me. "Mmm. Okay. Here it is: You don't know what you want."

I want a stiff drink, I think. I don't say it aloud.

I am afraid of being punished for touching the scissors.

I am still afraid of Gran.

I really am still a child. Or rather, I'm a child whenever I enter this room. Is it an enchantment? A curse? Or just an ordinary psychological burden that I bring with me when I come to visit, like those little kids at the church daycare where I work weekends, the ones who won't leave home without their stinky old stuffies then wonder why they can't make normal friends?

Granny continues without pause. "You want me to bring all these peoples back so you can ask them for advice. You don't trust self. You never have. You rely on others to see for you. To make choice for you. You don't need them."

"That's ridiculous. I just miss them."

"Oh?" Granny scoffed. "Tell me. After bringing the peoples back, what would you do with extra snip?"

"What extra snip?"

"So. The mufti did not explain, when he was spilling all secrets about my powers? Yes, I see. He told you things. Thinking he is *helping*. But never the whole story. Men, always this way. Always ignore what must come. See only now-things. Not future. Not unraveling of fate. Not the possible threads of time. Not the finished tapestry. Only now now now. You are too much like men. This country makes everyone a man."

I bite back my retort. Granny is always accusing people of being too male or too female. It is as if in her definitions the words are indicative, not of inborn or learned gender roles, but of arcane innate qualities that the old-world Kazakhs use other, more accurate, words to describe. A great deal of Granny's wisdom is likely lost in translation. And this ridiculous magic! I'm not able to decide if it is real or idiotic. Like prayer: Everyone says it works, but then they add that it's your own fault if it does not. So, how am I supposed to believe in old-world magic, even if the mufti explained that it was real? Was Grampa here? Was that a delusion? A vision? A ghost? Did I really see him? Did Gran? Where is the science in all of this? I want answers. I have always wanted answers. I got a whole master's degree searching for answers. Grampa showing up raised more questions than he answered, and this makes me angry, but the anger is wrapped around my mother and father who failed to teach me more than a few words of the Russian they spoke fluently, leaving me with only a single lousy tongue: English, which has power over nothing. My anger is pulled tighter knowing that even my parents could not speak a word of Kazakh, which Granny insists is the only true language of magic. The fierce anger is tied with a bow of secret shame. At the age of nineteen, I had actually been offered a scholarship to learn Kazakh at a summer program, but I had decided to rent a beach house with some friends instead; other American Kazakhs my age who had also stubbornly fought learning any language other than English. We thought we were clever to lie around drinking and getting high and doing everything possible to avoid learning the language of our grandparents. In other words, I made myself this ignorant. My ineptitude and impotence were self-inflicted. My anger lights on fire.

"Stick to the point, Granny. What's this extra snip?" I hear how shrill my voice is, and I grip the arm of Granny's floral sofa to calm myself. It wouldn't do to lose one's temper in here. I glance at the chess pieces. Am I safe because the set is full? Would she release the dog to capture me, instead?

But Granny is actually speaking: her soft eye focus is kindly, and she giggles as though she is a teenager confiding in a friend.

"The scissors cut threads of reality, huh? One thing is here, one thing goes away. One thing comes back. Extra snip cuts off something dear from your own life. Severs you from a thing that makes you human. Like payment for the work. Bill is due. And expensive always. So? What was to be for you, Salima? Would you hope scissor choose? Because it choose very random. Very dangerous to let scissor choose. Leads to despair."

"I… But… Mufti Isham didn't say anything about any extra snip. I didn't know! What's it going to do to me?" I said, too loud. "Can it do something without my knowing the rules? How can I stop it? Granny! What should I choose? How does this work?"

"Well-well. Surprise, surprise, young person." Granny takes another sip of tea. She smiles as if hot tea is the best thing in life. "Scissor doesn't care you did not know. Scissor take. You pay. Moon rise, you must decide. If you do not choose, scissor makes the choice. What will it be? Tasting of the sweets? Enjoying of music? Remembering of friends? Understanding of books? Of the poetry? Maybe you lose of art, the deep thinking, you want? Maybe you don't need sports?"

"But the scissors didn't even do anything permanent. You

just put everything back the way it was." I could not control the panic in my rising voice. "Grampa's gone! How can that even count?" I am behaving like a child. Gran was right.

"I know nothing," Granny says. Her voice betrays some sadness, as if she wishes it could be otherwise. "I did tell you put down, don't touch. I did warn. No one listens to old lady. Old, old Granny. I was great witch, once in a time. Used to be some special thing, peoples afraid, listened to Granny, came far far far to listen me, but now…?"

"Well, sure you told me to stop it, but…"

Granny's teacup clicks sharply onto the saucer and she stares into the cup.

"Give me peace. My medicine, I need this thing," Granny says. Then she shouts it. "Medicine! Nurse, nurse! Come!" She stares at me, and her expression changes to a frown, "Why you here, Umit? Why didn't you bring cake? I want cake. Cake!"

I rush to fetch the day-nurse from the office near the lobby. The hefty woman is reading a glossy magazine. She sighs, rises, and follows me back to the elevators, clucking, stinking of onions and garlic, her tiny silver cross glinting like hope in the middle of a broad expanse of age-spotted chest. The cross's extremities end in tumorous bulges, echoing the woman's enormous fingers and swollen ankles; but when she gets to Granny's rooms, she cleans the tea efficiently from Granny's housedress and locks the chess set deftly into its cabinet, pocketing the key before shooing me out of the room. "You young pipples are never any help to ze old pipples," she says, "Respect nussink. Care for nussink. Working old pipples nerves. Get out. Go be young somewheres else."

When moonrise comes, I am deep into a fifth of scotch, laughing with my grad-school friends about the man-bun our professor had attempted. My mind is far from Granny's warnings, and I don't notice when my phone rings an alert from the senior center. It isn't until morning, through a foggy hangover, that I discover that my grandmother has passed away.

All of Granny's possessions, including one antique chess set, have been bequeathed to the Senior Center. The Center kindly lets me reclaim the valuable set since I promise to replace it with a more durable model. The sewing basket, however, has vanished. It's possible that the Bulgarian day nurse stole it, but no one at the facility seems to care. No amount of cajoling or cash on my part has been able to recover it.

Until I can find the sewing kit, the chess set only sits on a glass coffee table in my studio apartment and gathers dust, waiting for me to grow old enough to forget what it means. In the meantime, I am taking a course in Kazakh and hoping for a miracle.

Mom of the Year

Gioia's new contact lenses flashed in a way only she could discern: incoming call. The iTrick messages could be seen only through special contacts. Brilliant for a busy celebrity.

Private number. Who'd call during a live taping? Her kids knew she was on the air. She'd been working toward this for ten years, and the coronavirus crap had really slowed things down. Thank fuck that was over. A red light lit on Camera Two. Gioia shifted for a better angle.

"The future of motherhood?" she repeated. The cameraman was shooting a close-up. They always turned out their feet when looking at her famous breasts. She cheated towards the camera. Give them what they want. The difference between con artist and celebrity was really so minimal. Her father, a Vegas card dealer, her mother a succubus of sorts, working night shifts—she'd picked it up genetically: the easy flash, the charm, the ever-shifting moral code. She fed on attention, money, and private jets. On promotional perks like this iTrick thing. Normal people flinched when a display lit up their retina. Gioia smiled mysteriously and read the alert; applied her most genuine smile.

"I'm hardly an expert, Ted."

Fifteen minutes, tops, and she could check the message.

"Millions of your fans would disagree," Ted prompted from his host-chair with one of the lecherous smiles she'd grown to expect from him over the years.

Just as she began to formulate a response, he dropped the subject. "Just tell the audience what your kids eat for lunch. Do you pack brown bags or do they have retro lunch boxes?"

Her eyes narrowed.

"They get fed on the set, of course," Gioia carefully replied.

The live studio audience responded with chuckles, amplified by sound fillers. One bozo yelled, *I'd like to pack Moniqqe's lunch* and got a security escort out the back door.

"Sorry for the interruption, Gioia."

"Not at all, Ted. My daughters have grown very strong dealing with unruly fans. What were we talking about?" The red light glowed on Camera One.

"Lunches?"

"The caterers of each show provide at least two organic options, Ted." She angled her torso slightly away from the lens to project sincerity. *Bring the audience to you, never go to them.* "And each child has a nutritionist to make sure they don't eat too much."

"Or too little, in Moniqqe's case."

"Or too little," she agreed. Media was probably the cause of Moniqqe's anorexia in the first place. The iTrick flashed again. Swag bags were Hollywood's dirtiest secret—make your first million and you get everything in advance of the masses. Free. God how she loved swag. "Ted, you know how it is on set; food available day and night, even now with all the new distancing rules and private carrels for Extras—that's a big change, huh? But there's still junk. It's really hard for kids to eat healthy at 3 a.m. when everyone else is scarfing M&Ms and Oreos to keep awake. I consider myself lucky they don't do drugs."

The studio lights were hot. She shifted uneasily, praying her skirt's leather seam didn't imprint on the back of her thigh. Shouldn't have mentioned 3 a.m. This was the most-viewed show on the planet.

Ted leaned on his armrest, his latest Botox injections too fresh to allow for raised eyebrows. Ready the defenses.

"Three a.m.? Isn't that a little late for a kid—?"

"It's only the teenagers." She gave her infamous bad girl pout. "At least I know where they are! They're not on video games. How many mothers can say that?"

"How many, indeed."

She was in for it. This host was known as The King of Scorn. Just answer the questions. Keep it simple. Stop looking down or he'll guess about the iTrick. How long was a segment these days? Five minutes? Three?

"So, six kids, six reality shows. When do you have time for *you?*"

Again she searched for mockery. He was good. Laugh it off.

"What mom has me-time? I take what I can get. You know, Ted, I went to a spa in Fiji last week—" She had been waiting for the opportunity to inject this after *E!* leaked it. Better the admission come from her. "I felt so guilty! But my kids agreed I should go. You give so much, you have to replenish, y'know?"

The studio audience seemed divided. Some jeered. Most applauded. The filter amplified the applause. The host held up a hand, amused.

"Jetting first-class from set to set doesn't seem to be taking its toll at all, Gioia. But I'm sure you've got a sweet private plane, don't you? You have to. Shows in DC, Arizona, two in New York City, LA, and Chicago. You're flying back and forth almost every day, so much stress between the virus and this wave of violence, and just look at you. Perfect as you were in *Perfection*."

"Thanks, Ted." She produced another smile. She was sick of the comment, actually. There wasn't an interviewer who ever said anything different. Still, it was nice they mentioned *Perfection*. That film was ten years ago. Meanwhile, her personal trainer was beginning to get snippy. Maybe it was time to fire him. "You forget that we all actually live in Wyoming."

"In a little log cabin."

She narrowed her eyes. "We have a nice home, Ted. It suits us." The screens showed their seventy-million-dollar estate, with graphics indicating the master bedroom in its aerie suite, a thousand yards from the closest child's room.

"I'm sure you and the kids love your time at home."

Popups showed the location of six nanny rooms.

"There's never enough of it."

"What about the fathers?"

Her hand jerked away from the coffee mug. What was Ted's game? This had been pre-negotiated. "The fathers?"

"You don't want to talk about them?"

She kept her face steady. "Well, Ted, three of them have new books out that I'm not plugging. You know as much as I do about the other three. Moniqqe's dad is the only one who wants anything to do with his kid, and I say fine. There are plenty of wonderful father figures on set. Geoffrey looks up to his director. Great role model. They play basketball together after some of the shorter shooting days." When the red light left Camera One, she let her face show her ire. *The fathers? How dare he?*

"It's a sensitive subject, I see." Ted smirked. "So, let's move onto something easier. How do you keep in shape? You don't look anything like a mom."

"What does a mom look like, Ted?" This interview was not going well. She hated talk of recent lifts—he knew that. The iTrick flashed again. Third call.

"Well, *my* mom looks like a million bucks." He acknowledged the smattering of applause in the studio audience. "Tell me, how hard was it to develop a reality TV show for a six-month-old?"

"Not hard at all." The comment escaped before she sensed the trap. "I mean—the network executives approached me. I put up a fight; nothing would have pleased me more than being a stay-at-home. Even now, I ache whenever he reaches for me. But all my kids need me, you know, Ted? I can't play favorites."

A voice from the audience screamed *You sold your baby! You monster!* Gioia frowned for a split second before realizing her camera was on.

"My children are all extremely talented," she said, tossing her hair. "Moniqqe's show was the highest ranked reality show for three years running."

"Let's talk about Woo for another second. This is going to sound crass, but the audience is dying to know." Gioia waited patiently through the applause and was ready. "Just how much did they offer you for the newborn?"

"Ted. When they told me the details—a show inner city kids could watch to understand what it's like to be a teen parent—well, the humanitarian angle meant more to me than the money. All those kids saved from unwanted pregnancies."

"But the money must be good; I mean, to place your kid with a random teenager and let the nation watch how it comes out?"

"Ted." She gave a luscious pout. "The teen-parents are vetted. Woo is never in any danger whatsoever. The teens are all post-pubescent and they truly love babies. I mean, they want their own, you know? It's educational. How dare you suggest I did it for the money?"

"It's what they pay me for." He grinned. She could see his age in the tightness of his cheekbones. Sixty if he was a day. He'd be retired soon, thrown to pasture—much like her, she guessed, though the unfairness of gender still galled her. Men in their 50s were distinguished; while women in their 50s were disposable. How was she supposed to stay in the limelight? One day, maybe Hollywood could rediscover her as a fierce old crone. But for now, she had to flirt with the producers until it was her turn again.

Youth doesn't comprehend. They want room to grow; kick aside the geezers. They don't understand their own destiny, that day you wake up middle-aged! Ted should have been a kindred spirit. His twins were early YouTubers! At least her six were paid.

Ted wasn't done.

"I have a clip from *Tenement*, Gioia."

This was a surprise; hopefully nothing awful happened yesterday. She'd seen most of the season. What would he show? Woo strapped to the baby seat in front of the TV while the girl chatted on the phone? The awful episode where the girl let her drunk uncle toss him in the air? Nothing could be worse than that one.

A screen came to life. She sensed focus tighten on her camera. *Scenes from next season, rough cut,* the text read. She suppressed an angry shout; legal was supposed to vet these. Rough cuts were never, never supposed to get out. Damn that new publicist.

There was Woo, giggling in the bathtub. He loved water. Little Aquarius. She felt her face soften. What a great little dude. Never cried, just took whatever was coming. The girl was squirting something blue and viscous into the tub, what was that? Some new bath product placement? The water was turning blue, and Woo was laughing. Gioia sat up, stunned, one step ahead of the film. "No!" she said, just as the girl dunked the baby's head in the tub, completely submerging him. It was so shocking that the picture wavered—the camera operator must have been surprised as well. The studio audience was in cacophony: some yelling that Gioia had drowned her baby, some yelling at Ted, some at the girl who'd done the dunking. Onscreen, the girl scooped Woo out of the blue water, laughing at his now-blue hair. Woo was screeching as never before, the camera operator's cursing was bleeped, the girl laughed and held the baby out to the lens—then the screen went to black. Ted did not miss a beat.

"So, what do you—?"

But Gioia was already doing damage control.

"My God. A lot of people are getting fired over this." She saw Ted open his mouth and quickly went on. "But I don't blame that girl, Ted. The fault is with the viewers. They want to see bad things happen. The fans write in ideas so horrible, you can't imagine. They never consider the life of that little child. My tiny son." She let her eyes well up, knowing her mascara would hold. Ted loved waterworks; maybe he'd ease up. "You see why *Tenement* is so important? All over this country, teenagers having babies treat them like dolls or toys. Big companies make these insane products like poop-shaped soap you can eat, or paints for computer screens, and little kids are expected to use their judgment. They have no judgment, Ted. They're babies."

"Your kids do reality shows for the good of society?" Ted's voice was dry as burnt meat.

"Your words, not mine." Gioia's iTrick flashed again.

The audience rustled in anticipation.

"Here's the stats, folks. Moniqqe is making two million per episode, provided she does nudity; Tasha is making three mil, same thing. Geoffrey gets six hundred thousand, but shoots daily; that grosses to three mil a week, same as his sister. Of course, his medical bills probably net him less. Sabine is making only thirty-thousand, but she's new, right? And her show hasn't taken off."

"Bookworms don't sell." Gioia sighed. Why couldn't she play along like her sisters? Tasha wasn't even a lesbian! Why did Sabine think it was enough to sit in the corner, reading books? The only people who watched her show were channel-surfers and Japanese pervs. Dig the Catholic Schoolgirl uniform; that sort of thing. This was Gioia's third attempt to sell Sabine; the girl just wasn't into it.

"Myanmar, on the other hand," she prompted.

"Myanmar will never go hungry," Ted quipped. "Your idea of tying him to the country he was named for was a stroke of genius. Even I watch that show. Makes my Tuesday. Little five-year-old, telling off grownups? Hilarious. I loved the episode where Myanmar told the cashier she was slow and fat. Oh my god, I nearly fell off my chair."

"Well." She smiled, *easy now*, she'd gotten over the hurdle with the King of Scorn, slow and steady. "The woman stood there eating Skittles instead of ringing up his purchases. Granted he could hardly see over the counter, but that's … that's probably a lawsuit, actually." She let Ted join in her laughter. "I like that show best of all," she said, working the revelation like a striptease, "because it's just *loaded* with irony."

Ted turned to Camera One. Gioia took the opportunity to yawn and stretch her wrists in little circles; she rewarded the audience with a coy wink.

Ted was saying, "…*Capitalism*—set in DC, little Myanmar X gets a million dollars a week to spend any way he wants, and any money left at the end of the week goes to charity in the country of Myanmar, where you get to see what good it does. He's a disgusting little brat, and the monks save hundreds of lives. It's brilliant."

"I wouldn't call him disgusting." Gioia beamed into her camera. "I think he's delightfully honest. A breath of fresh air."

"Sure, but you don't have to live with him," said Ted.

"I visit him every week, and when his show isn't taping, we spend a lot of time at the house. How often do you see your kids,

Ted?"

"Let's talk about the baby," he replied. "How often do you see *him?*"

"Ted," she said, summoning up all the focus her morning yoga Zoom had given her, "I just won Mom of the Year from three different magazines. I hardly think that someone whose kids call him—"

"Don't believe everything you read," Ted interrupted. "Congratulations on your terrific awards. Three in one year. Amazing. I wonder if your kids would have voted with the judges?"

"I love my kids," she replied. Inside, she was quivering.

"You've passed the baton. How does that feel, Gioia?"

"Everything I do, I do for my kids."

"And would you say they all return that love?"

A deep-seated celebrity instinct told her something big, raw, and painful was about to be revealed. Even the audience caught on and tittered.

"We are a very close family, Ted."

She didn't know about the screen that showed Sabine pacing in the green room like an angry panther.

"We'll be back after the break," Ted told Camera Two, "with a little surprise for the three-time Mom of the Year." Both cameras winked off, and everyone slipped Covid masks on.

"And we're out. Three minutes." From over in the corner, a P.A. about the same age as Moniqqe stepped forward. "Is there anything I can get you, ma'am? Coffee? Pressed juice, water?"

Gioia was scanning texts, so furious she could barely hear. From Geoffrey: *Don't talk about Sabine.* From Moniqqe: *S on warpath.* From her agent: *Sabine's suing you. Call Frank.*

What an ungrateful little monster. That's what she'd take to the tabloids: *Mom of the Year Pities Ungrateful Middle Child.* Someone would buy it. Fox maybe. CNN was certainly going to run something along the opposite front: *Oppressed Child Star Sues Mom of the Year.*

Hair and Makeup arrived wielding brushes of various sizes. They smoothed, blotted, and cooed, while Ted read the welcome-back recap in close-up. Three of the four techies faded into the background, and Gioia had a quick gulp of water from a coffee cup. The lingering makeup artist with her surgically altered cat ears pressed a tissue to Gioia's lip and dabbed a touch of Blushing Bride on her cheekbones before leaping silently away, leaving only the cheering audience, the radiant celebrity, and the beaming host when the light illuminated on the top of Camera Two.

"So Gioia," Ted began, satisfied yet hungry, the smile of the hyena who has taken down the zebra. "Let's talk about your daughters. What sort of role model are you?"

Gioia took a slow breath. Turnabout, she guessed. Her mom's ghost flitted around the studio, calling her *ungrateful.*

"I was raised by sitters. Didn't do me a bit of harm."

"That's not what your memoir says."

"Authors write to sell books, Ted. Memoirs are just stories." The audience was restless, choosing sides. She exhaled yoga-style. Inhaled through her nose. Plastered a wide, grateful smile over her fear. "My mom was a role model. From her, I learned to be strong and self-sufficient. Independent."

Ted cut her off. "What about your dad?"

"What do you want me to say, Ted?" Her voice dripped sarcasm, but tears were edging close. "My dad was an old fat man

I saw every other weekend. We went to the zoo. A guy in a casino uniform and his skinny kid. He rode me on his shoulders so he could text his bookie between animals. My childhood was fine."

"You don't sound fine."

"I'm telling you I'm fine."

"But Sabine isn't fine."

Sabine must have gone to the tabloids. Like mother, like daughter. Gioia recalled the night her own mother finally deigned to watch *Perfection*. The message on her answering machine two months after the movie's release, "If I had boobs like that I would've tried to make it in the biz myself." How angry she'd been at her mother; the nasty way she'd gotten her revenge. The tabloids loving her shame.

Ted leaned into her. "A daughter taking you to court. Again."

She smiled mildly, straightened her spine and addressed the studio audience.

"Sabine is a smart kid," she started, "but first and foremost, a kid. How many of you are parents?"

Strong applause.

"Well, then you're familiar with the constant tug-of-war for attention. This lawsuit is just another attempt at getting mom-time. Stealing me from her siblings. *This is what kids do*—they fight over parental attention. All kids want more. Haven't you ever been to a mall? Some kid is always screaming *I hate you dad, why do you have to work all the time.*" She was beginning to relax, the tension of the past few minutes easing out of her shoulders, when her iTrick flashed again. She had to read this newest message before Ted broke more bad news.

"When was the last time you were in a mall? Or any of us?"

Ted was trying to take her off her grandstand. Gioia would have none of it. Folks at home would believe she sincerely felt awkward about revealing these 'dirty secrets' on air. As she intended them to.

"I lost Moniqqe's emancipation suit, but I fought hard. That nudity clause was entirely her own doing. What mother would sell her daughter's sexuality like that? Courts agreed. When Tasha followed in her footsteps, I fought it again. Same with Geoffrey. Those legal battles cost more than just money. It's hurtful to sit in a court of law listening to your kid telling a judge they don't want you filtering their reviews. Saying they know better than you do."

"They won."

"They won. But as you know, Ted, all three of them came crawling back to me within two years, begging me to take them on as formal business clients. Know what they said? Without me, they were just stars; together, we were a dynasty. A dynasty, Ted. You know the power of that word here in Hollywood? It's voodoo."

"But Sabine—" Ted began.

"With Sabine I tried an entirely different tactic," Gioia said. Her trademark smile didn't belong in this monologue, but she threw it on anyway. "We were so tight when Sabine was a baby. It was with the best intentions that I promised I would grant her a no-contest emancipation when she turned 15—this was brand-new at the time—in exchange for her signing me as exclusive manager. Add her to the dynasty, as it were. Lawsuits kill me. I didn't want to go through another one. It's easier for me to give the kids their freedom, and work within an established contract. Who knows what a mother's role should be—but a manager?

That's a very clear, specific job description. I love my kids; I don't want to bicker with their lawyers."

It was Ted's turn to look surprised. It made the skin under his eyes look baggy.

"So Sabine's already emancipated?"

"Has been for three months."

The studio audience was hers. Gioia could feel it as if it were a physical thing; a warm mink blanket or fox-fur coat. Ted must have felt it too, because his questions grew clumsy.

"So, if this lawsuit isn't about emancipation, what's it—?"

"Honestly, Ted, I'm not sure." She hoped she sounded sincere. This hostile interview might result in the best publicity she'd have for the next few months. There was a quick commercial break, and while Hair & Makeup fussed, Gioia managed a look at her iTrick. It wasn't Frank.

U R A BITCH.

Sabine.

She wanted to reply, to assuage, or at least acknowledge that her daughter was in pain—but there wasn't time. Ted welcomed back his viewers, and she felt electric tension in the air.

"Well, let's find out together, shall we, Gioia?" said Ted. He bolstered the audience into a rousing cheer. "Who sues the Mother of the Year? Audience, give it up for Sabine X!"

The red light on her camera glowed. They wanted that reaction shot. Gioia did her best to give them nothing: she parted her lips as she'd been trained, breathed deep into her lungs without letting her shoulders rise, and let the emotional shock and despair ride out on her breath. Her eyes prickled a little, but she closed them very deliberately, forcing the moisture to redistribute. The audience rose to its feet, howling and whistling. Hungry. Gioia didn't know whether they were hoping for Sabine to be destroyed or her; she wasn't sure this audience much cared, so long as somebody died.

Every eye was on the blue curtain held aside by a gaunt P.A. who would be invisible to the cameras. Then there was Sabine. Though dressed in a chic designer suit, she moved as if she was wrapped in diaphanous fabrics that needed time to catch a breeze.

"Hi, Mom," she said.

"Hi, honey," Gioia replied.

When had Sabine stopped slouching? Her daughter's hair was black and glossy, exotically beautiful, and Gioia unconsciously touched her own blonde locks and wished she hadn't succumbed to pressure. The gray was just too noticeable though. She couldn't dye her hair more than once every two weeks or it lost its luster. While *Struttin'* played on the overhead and the audience screamed, her daughter sat down in a newly added seat and was fitted with a mic. Gioia saw the way the silk blouse (nice choice) fell tight against her daughter's waist. Gioia recalled staring at the mirror in her own mother's house after school while the sitter watched soaps on TV, staring and wishing her body would hurry up and develop the power that movie star bodies always had. You looked at a glossy magazine and the women made you feel powerful. They were beautiful in a way that gave you hope. *That could be me, if only I could find the right clothes. Cut my hair right. If we had money. If only...* She'd loved the glossies, and there was Sabine, looking like she was clipped right from the pages of *Cosmo*.

A bittersweet tang rose in the back of Gioia's throat. *I made you, girl. You grew in my body. Every last bit of you—ankles, eyebrows, even that gorgeous long neck—every bit of you was part of me once.* The taste was sorrow. The taste was pride. No wonder kids traded small skin grafts with their best friends. They wanted to entirely own themselves and they innately knew that they never would, so they controlled their own destruction.

Your body is never entirely your own, no matter how you abuse it.

How many times had she said that to her kids? Or to herself, in the mirror? The public owned them all. They might as well make some money.

Gioia watched Ted settle the audience. Sabine stared straight ahead. She had always hated being on camera. Always hated publicity, attention, fame. That was her whole problem, thought Gioia. She refused to play the game. Her siblings loved their shows. Sure, they went overboard, and they had their problems: Tasha's stalkers, Moniqqe's anorexia, Geoffrey's occasional broken rib, but in general, they were good kids who loved what they did. That's why she'd got those Mom of the Year awards, after all. There weren't many kids who were happy, so obviously happy—with millions of views of every single episode—and whose happiness could so overtly be credited to their mom.

"So, Gioia," Ted said. "Ladies. Our producers thought maybe we could save Sabine a fortune in legal fees. We thought you two might want to talk your issues out in person. Air them, as the case may be."

The audience guffawed, then fell swiftly silent. They were geared up; fist fights, hair-pulling, waterworks. They wanted it all.

To Gioia's shock, Sabine began seriously.

"My mother doesn't talk," she said. "She performs."

Sabine turned her head like an owl noting prey. It was strange to be trapped in a chair six feet from her daughter. Too far for intimacy but close enough to examine. Such hooded, golden eyes. The gaze was familiar, identical to her own from twenty years ago. It hurt to see the similarity, hurt more to feel the age difference. She was old, her time past. Sabine's time yet to come. Her job as mom was to listen, and instead she was plotting a countersuit. Public opinion would be on Sabine's side, she realized, just as it had been on Moniqqe's, and on hers when she sued her own parents. It didn't matter what the issues were, nor who was right. Adults were, after all, thwarted children themselves.

Even parents had been kids first—and had been kids longer. Parenting was madness.

"Sabine. A lawsuit? So passé."

"I had to get your attention, Mom."

"I don't abuse you. I don't exploit you. You have the power to fire your own people and quit your own show. You can't say I made bad choices for you." She could see the expression of bliss on Ted's face and hated him for it, but she couldn't stop. This was about a mother talking sense to her daughter. "What do you lack, Sabine? You've got a tutor I hired away from Harvard, a personal trainer I use myself, the best nutritionist *in the world,* two personal assistants, a dresser, a stylist, a Juilliard-trained piano teacher, and an ex-ABT dance teacher. Hell, you've even got your own shrink. What more does a kid need, Sabine? More money?"

"More family time."

The red light flicked on. Gioia knew her camera was focused tight, but her jaw fell open. What kind of primitive, backwards, crazy, insane, stupid, pre-feminist, pre-modern, cave-dwelling shit was this? *I need my family?* Jesus H. Christ. Most fifteen-year-olds were running, *flying,* away from their parents. Gioia took the empty coffee mug off the table and pretended to drink from it. She had to gain control of the scene, that was all. She had to maintain the appearance of harmony for the next three minutes. They could hash the details later, break dishes if they had to, but for now, she needed to reduce the damage.

"Please, Sabine," she coaxed. What could she say? How could she beg? What on Earth would sway a girl who wanted her *mommy*? "I'm so sorry. You and me, we're artists, sugar. Artists have to hurt; it's the way of the world. I love you; give me another chance."

It was exactly the wrong thing to say.

Gioia's heart sank as she watched Sabine's lovely lips release her sharp, mirthless laugh across the room, where it sank echoless among her waiting fans. Red light again. Turned out feet. Damn that cameraman and his close-ups. Gioia folded her hands into a terrified knot. Squeezed.

"Saw that film, Mom." Bile dripped from her daughter's voice. "And by the way, you sucked in it."

The camera was broadcasting Gioia's shock, as well as the expression that briefly, fleetingly, had crossed her face: the realization that yes, Sabine was right, she'd accidentally quoted a line from one of her early films. The line was to a lover who'd been discovered to have a second life painting nudes. At the end of the movie, the lover had painted a portrait of Gioia and placed himself in the work. It was a stupid movie, and not a single critic had liked it. It was clear to Gioia that her daughter was smarter than she was; that the mention of *family time* had been a test to see if Gioia could stop thinking of her own career for longer than a second. From her daughter's expression, Gioia saw that she had failed.

And the irony was that Gioia remembered doing the same thing to her own mother before cutting her off completely.

How was work, Mom?

It was a test. Little Gioia had always hoped her mom would say *Work was fine, dear, thanks for asking. How was your day?* But in reality, her mother only talked-talked-talked about how excruciating her day had been. By the time she got around to saying *but now I'm home, sweetie, and I'm glad to see you,* Gioia had often cursed her mother out and ran crying from the room. And here was Sabine. Waiting.

Gioia looked at Ted. Ted her savior. Her demon. The show had to be over soon. Had to wrap in a minute. His ratings would be through the roof. He'd broken a story; he'd caught her expressions, hell, he could make a million easy just by selling the frozen screenshot of the moment her daughter first called her *mom*. He should pity her, should see they were members of the same sorry parent union, victims of the same lousy crime. She lifted her hands his way, helpless, empty.

We're old, they said silently. *If we let them, they'll kill us before we die.*

And the old coot actually felt sorry for her. He let the whole thing wind down, explained to the disappointed audience that time had run out; shrugged off his angry producer (who'd emerged waving from the hermetically sealed booth), and quite smoothly wrapped up the show with a final ad-lib, ignoring the vitriol scrolling down his Teleprompter.

"Well, Gioia," he said, "I wish you all the best. You certainly put us all to shame: managing six kids' blossoming careers. It's no wonder you have a tense moment every once in a while. Who wouldn't? I'm dying to see what happens to baby Woo in *Tenement*, and I'm sure the whole nation will be watching to see who Myanmar trash-talks next week. Mother-of-the-Year, it was great talking to you. Hope to see you on the big screen again soon. Sabine X, thank you for coming on my show and good luck with your future."

"Thank you, Ted," Sabine muttered. She looked robbed of something. A young fifteen. Lost. A child, still. Gioia felt sorry for her. It was all she could do not to wrap her arms around her little girl and cuddle her. How quickly they grow up.

"It's been a pleasure."

"Don't mention it, Ted. It was such a wonderful surprise to see my daughter."

Sabine raised her eyebrows, and Gioia had to look away. Sometimes she disgusted herself.

"Always great to have you on my show."

From over in the corner, the black-garbed girl stepped forward to give the cue.

"And…we're out. Thanks, everyone. Great show!" she said.

Sabine rose from her chair, and with all the ferocity of a thwarted teen, ripped the mic from her lapel and threw it onto the seat. Gioia tried to apologize, but her daughter was gone. Ted looped on a paper mask and vanished after her into the green room, presumably to talk her into a solo follow-up.

Gioia just sat. Lights went to dim, then fluorescents

illuminated the space so it appeared like what it was: a cheaply carpeted office with rows of risers and distanced folding chairs. A lousy illusion. She toyed with her hair, half-remembering that she looked stupid as a blonde. Someone from the departing audience usually asked for her autograph, but coronavirus measures made this group leave in pods as quickly as possible and without speaking. She blinked at her iTrick to view the messages. All those words and not one of them said, *Thanks mom, I love you mom, you're the greatest…*

"Gioia!" Ted was waving his own fancy new device in the air. "Great show. How would you like another segment later in the season? I can give you a five-minute exclusive in three weeks. The Trump girl backed out. You can do some damage control on *Bookworm*."

Instinct, honed by years of talking to producers, lent Gioia the absolute knowledge that the tide had turned. This wasn't about filling a spot. He wanted her, was courting her. Might pay for an exclusive. That crazy daughter of hers had made her a hot news item again. The vagaries of Hollywood. She made a mental note to send Sabine a gift certificate to…to… whatever store the girl wanted. She'd ask someone. Meanwhile, Ted was waiting. She could sense his saliva pooling.

"Can't, love," she smoothly replied.

He was the shark, and she, the diver safely—infuriatingly—in the cage.

"Crazy-busy. Gotta run. But do call my agent."

He stood there, furious, hand hovering mid-air.

While the audience wranglers paid the handful of audience fillers their cash, the director approached Gioia and made that stupid gesture that said she was used to touching people, but these days it wasn't allowed. Gioia looked the director up and down: mid-thirties, short-cropped hair, Malibu tan, tantric tattoo, six-pack abs, the fancy Tesla face shield that was so hard to get, and no wedding ring.

"Um, Gioia. Thanks. I'd just like to say that we're all amazed that you can do it. Six kids. You're an inspiration."

Gioia bared her fangs. "You've got the same equipment, hon. It's a choice."

She would never have been in these waters if it weren't for the sharks. She let the director remove the mic, then Gioia pushed up from the seat and slipped easily out the door, her mask dangling from her ear.

Decorated

If I never see another fat cell counter, it will be too soon.

I long for salami sandwiches on fluffy crusty bread. Cheese, hot from an oven. I want to leave filthy dishes to soak in a tub of soapy water. I would like to have a cat curl up on my lap and amuse me by glaring smugly at the dog that wants to share in my attention. I want to stare into a fire and let it burn.

Deep space tents around this ship—and these days it irritates, like a scratchy black blanket full of pinprick moth holes. Sure, the stars "wink and beckon and glitter with distant fire," as the old song goes, but their temptations are the stuff of mythological sirens. All teeth and lies and death, impatiently waiting for someone to slip up and forget where they are for the briefest moment. I hate them, every last one of them, every sister to every binary and every dwarf who laughed at me uncharted until I captured them all. They're still laughing, even though they are entrapped now on maps that bear my name, watermark, and voiceprint.

As I am trapped by my own success.

For decades, I followed my talents, my childhood dreams, climbing the ladder of achievement as defined by mentors and governments and strangers. I allowed myself to be flattered into ever more responsibility, nodding and smiling my way through ceremonies I hated, to accept commissions I didn't want to places I feared to go. I winked at the admiral each time she pinned another moon to my collection. She winked back, despite the possibility of our camaraderie being noticed by the media, knowing that in mere hours we would both be plastered and our drinks would slosh across the shiny bar and we would revel in the lovely tug of gravity, however slight. My best friend and I would slur in parallel harmonies about the stars, their beautiful fields of light, and how flying through them is a gift that few receive, and perhaps some aliens of the proper gender would buy all the balderdash and then I would have some release even though I would be forced to whisper all night how I value this, value them, value my life, my adventures.

Few would ever know I was lying.

Truth is, I don't want to be ship's captain anymore.

You can find the same tranquility floating on your back in a deep pool of water or other viscosity, attain serenity simply by looking up at the stars through the nocturnal atmosphere of nearly any planet. Same same.

So why abandon everyone you love for cycles at a time?

Why the rigor?

I want a lover to stay for a week.

I want to be selfish.

I want to breathe as deeply as I feel like breathing. I want all the air to myself.

No one can know this.

Tomorrow when we dock at Cyrilian 4, I will stand straight, shake hands firmly with President Duarte. I will salute where I must. I will keep my eyes flinty and look only at her forehead. Nothing will reach my core, and I will never remove the facemask.

***

The metal shudders beneath my hands, sends me careening from the wall of the control room. I push off a flat part of the opposite wall and scoot back across the chamber to the array, where I am informed that one of the security satellites orbiting the station has identified the attacker as a Blue Agate ship and destroyed it.

My stomach clenches.

I once met an adjunct CEO of Blue Agate at an intercorporate networking function my bosses were hosting, something with exotic disinhibitors, and Tai, the Admiral, and I spent many a delicious hour with the entertainers, a troupe of poetic dancers—some, if I recall correctly, with multiple, multihued appendages. Were Tai and I enemies now? The array informs me that Blue Agate was recently acquired by the competition, a conglomerate called Nebula Cloud. Such are the ways of business.

In any event, the ship is already destroyed. There hadn't even been time for my heart rate to double between the initial attack and completely calm skies. I look at the display: shards of carbon steel swirling in dust clouds away from the drone's point of impact. My eyes glisten for the lives of the probable friends of my one-time acquaintance, and I know for a fact that I have become unstable.

I am too old for my position. I no longer value the lives I am saving over those lives lost in saving them. I no longer feel that my discovery of a world is equal to an improvement for that world, and I wonder if the word discovery should even be used in the context of something that predates our knowledge of it. I have begun to fear the fragile future that Halifax and I are protecting. I want to watch a green bean sprout from soil under a bare sun. I'm tired of recycling my urine. I don't love the color black anymore.

***

The pod holding Halifax 1 has a blinking green light. I stare at it as if stoned on leaf sugar until a stupid pop song from some memorable risk-fest in my adolescence invades my thoughts with sappy lyrics of lost love and rediscovered solitude and begins to irritate my brain with parallel beats. I find my hand drumming on the shell of the pod and pull away with an automatic mutter of apology to the insensate Halifax. Everything reminds me of something else these days. Nothing is itself anymore. Another few verses of the old song play themselves out in my mind, and I palm the pod's sensory panel and watch the counters flicker to life and the time set itself to twelve. The light glows solid green.

I have twelve hours until Halifax is thawed. When they emerge, they will be captain. I will be gone.

***

The rest of the crew sleeps in cryo, and as I float past each one, I enter a comment on their clip. *Halifax 4, your efforts with Dr. Wirthell were commendable. Halifax 12, keep playing mah-jongg, you are getting better. Halifax 34, thank you for allowing me to taste the sroughlette you brought back from Stylos' moon, that was generous of you and I will never forget the feeling of eating starlight.* It takes two hours to coast the entire line of pods on my errand. It is a sentimental thing to do, but I want them to know I knew them each as individuals as well as the collective. I want them to recall me as a good captain.

***

I don't know why that matters.

***

I write a resignation to the Admiral, apologizing for missing the forthcoming ceremony on Cyrilian 4. I recommend Halifax and give my full confidence to them. I explain nothing of my reluctance; leave no room for misinterpretation of my words. I do not mention our long friendship. She will know without my saying that I would have loved to raise a glass to her one last time. I set the message to post in eleven hours, just before Halifax fully wakes.

***

The airlocks wait at the end of the ship near the shuttles.

I wonder if the drones will try to save me. I wouldn't put it past them. I shut down the protection systems, starting with the shields. It is a gaping security glitch I have never understood that you have to lower the shields to jettison even a single cube of space trash. The timer to restart gives me pause. How long will it take to override the safeties on the third airlock? Will half an hour be enough? I err on the side of caution and give myself forty minutes, though some deep-seated responsible part of me winces for even this brief amount of peril I'm putting the Halifax in. Not that there have been any real threats to this ship in the last three years. Plenty of hapless pirates, random space junk, rerouted asteroids, rumors of mythical incorporeal creatures—the only real worry we have left in space are free-floating biohazards. Virus clouds, bioweapons that no one swept after they did their thing, death-matter. I set the timer for thirty-five minutes: my crew will be fine.

That is, the new captain will be fine.

This ship has a top of the line, SpaceXVI triple airlock with hinging doors and redundant air feed in case of entrapment. I need to get to the second airlock and override the safeties on the third. This will take about twenty-five minutes of coding and a steel will. It will also take a steady hand and monk-like endurance; the first airlock is cold, but it is freezing beyond the second, and I am wearing only the usual flight suit. Why waste a spacesuit if I am planning to die anyway? Halifax will need them.

***

I am through the tenth line of code, teeth chattering and fingers stiffening, when the walls shudder again and I stop everything in accordance with my training, and automatically check with security. Again the ship has been attacked. Again the drones have taken out the offending vessels, three of them; negligible pirate ships working together to try to take a big payload. Imagine my surprise when the airlock behind me swings open to admit a small lavender-skinned alien.

"Identify yourself," I say. My weapon is trained on it before I even consciously register its appearance. Lavender-skinned humanoid. Quadrupedal. Something the Admiral would have dubbed a Centauri—she of the mythological puns. No odor, which is strange for a mammalian from any planet. Large orbs for eyes, ringed with elaborate lashes. Small furry ears and a long line for a mouth. This alien might have been designed by a bioarchitect to make one think of cuddly pets, comfort, and loyalty.

"I am Morry," says a soft, trusting voice. "Ally. No danger."

I don't buy it, for didn't the surface of the vessel shake? That meant lasers or matter manipulations. Projectile weapons. Still, this does not look like your usual pirate. I swallow a lump of guilt for lowering the shields. "Morry" raises four arms in a sign of surrender and transparency. I glower and do not let down my guard. This Morry moves more quickly than my eyes can follow, freezes, then moves again. It is disconcerting, almost as if Morry is blinking in and out of existence. I don't like it.

"No weapon," Morry says, four arms higher now, and also longer than I thought they were before. "Nothing to danger you."

"State your purpose," I demand. I have fallen back on my training. It's automatic after fifty years. I don't think. I act.

"No purpose," Morry replies immediately. "Safety. Please.

Refuge."

All I want is to jettison myself into space. Morry's huge eyes beg me to wait. Morry needs me, but Morry picked the wrong day, the wrong human. I have been fighting my sense of duty all morning, have already broken many rules—why not also this one? Why not discard my basic humanity? If I plan to die anyway, what is stopping me from shooting a defenseless Morry?

My hesitation allows Morry to redefine the situation. Morry becomes translucent, and the minute I notice this, I know what "Morry" is: a pheenomorph. Not much is known about them for none have been recovered dead or alive. The myths call them deadly, living deep in space, attracted by the exhaust of starships. Able to penetrate walls by shapeshifting. Plasma shields supposedly block them. Conveniently. So you never see them on stations or ships or in cities. The theory is that they absorb carbon from living creatures and inanimate objects in order to replenish the carbon they lose by shifting. All I know is that if any of these tales are true, I am in mortal danger, my ship and Halifax are at risk, and it is not a thought, it is an instinct that has me pounding the airlock open far too violently, with too much adrenaline to allow for clear thinking. My training responds without thought—my duty is to my ship and my crew.

The pheenomorph moves sluggishly closer, arms extended as if to grab me, or maybe embrace me. It phases in trippy static-filled jerks and I wonder if they move faster in the frigidity of space. My brain is on overdrive, panicked: perhaps in the higher temperatures in the main body of the ship, the pheenomorph would be further slowed. I can only hope the effect is a quick one;

a torpid pheenomorph should be easier to destroy.

I speed back into the warmer climate of the first airlock. The pheenomorph follows, shifting into a semi-transparent cloud of atoms. Projectiles will be useless against it, and lasers would likely also do no damage. It does, in fact, appear to move more slowly in the warmer air, and I duck into the main body of the ship and reach for the first thing my fingers find—the spacesuit I left on the hook when I began my walk into oblivion.

I grab the spacesuit and use it like a net, throwing it wildly over the pheenomorph cloud. Most of it is caught inside and I speak the voice commands to heat the suit—I am sorry there is no helmet attached to it, but the pheenomorph does not seem to be able to escape the heat—in any event, I continue to wave the suit with the alien inside like a kid with a weird kite that refuses to catch the wind. I must look insane, trying to gain purchase to keep the pheenomorph within the rapidly heating suit. Gravity would be so useful, but I am doing my best. At last the swirls that have been attempting to reconnect with the main through the suit float lifeless in various directions like some strange seedpod exploded by a freakish wind. I clip the helmet to the suit, and ratchet the heat up to full. I'll cook this thing. Nothing is going to harm my crew.

**

The full Halifax is awake, all of them at first surprised at the change in schedule then charmed by the notes I had written. They assume I woke them early to help deal with the invasion. I allow the myth to survive, quietly delete my outgoing mail in its timed queue. They hail me as a hero, passing the empty spacesuit back and forth, marveling at the soot stains as if they are looking at a headless Jabberwock. We are all careful not to touch the interior. Science needs it.

We arrive at Cyrillian 4 six hours ahead of schedule. Crew loyalty—as well as having all lives saved and our ship saved and an unkillable mysterious alien dead and new cells or granules or whatever-the-hell captured for study, well, it was a combination of factors, let's say. It allowed the Admiral to pin yet another moon to my lapel. It is she who winks first this time, and, oh what the hell, I wink back though my throat is raw from repeating descriptions of the pheenomorph to various corporate heads on various recording devices. I do not feel well now, not well at all. I hear my own raspy voice tell the Admiral I won't be joining her for our usual drink. Many details have been omitted in my version of the capture, and I do not think I can deflect my friend's questions while wearing this extra moon. Meanwhile, societal agitation surrounding pheenomorphs has risen given this new strong evidence they can evade our plasma shields.

I have planned to take a few days off, see how I feel after floating in a pool of liquid on a planet with gravity and dirt and naturally occurring flora. Perhaps I will feel renewed and ready to run from moon to moon again; it has happened before. Perhaps I will sink to the bottom until my lungs burn for oxygen, knowing that here at least, I can burst to the surface and emerge, entirely suitless, body parts flailing like the tentacles of the unnamed aliens of Banga 14, gasping up atmosphere greedily, in unlimited quantities, sucking it in with tears or laughter. No need to control my emotions, much less my intake of breath. No one but a traveler like me appreciates the randomness of scent on one's own home planet—the way you are frequently surprised by olfactory change. "Sour milk!" one might say with a shock. Or, "Eww, what's in the garbage?" Or, "Oh, what sweet honeysuckle." On our way to the Navy Lodge, Halifax 6 says they will miss me, and I respond with a little laugh that I will miss them too.

It is best if they think so.

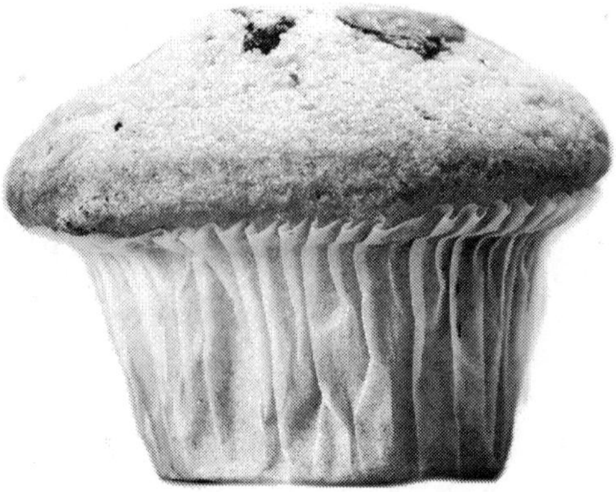

Wild Witch Treats

Once there was a woman who rode her bicycle to work every day. She passed a long string of shabby row houses, a few parking lots, a strip mall, a Walmart, and finally got to an office complex where no one greeted her, and no one was ever nice to her, and she worked there all day. Every evening, she mounted her bike and took herself home.

One morning, she rode past the row houses, passed two of the parking lots, and where the third one had been the day before, she slowed her pace because there was something new and impossible.

There was a bakery in the center of a grassy field with a glossy granite path that led directly to the glass double-door. The bakery had not been there the night before.

Helen's bicycle came to a complete stop. She slipped from the seat to stand straddling the bar.

"Wild Witch Treats," she read aloud. "Finally get what you

deserve."

Delicious tingles crawled down both arms to her hands, where they rested on the handlebars. Was her bike sparkling? Were her shoes brighter?

Wild Witch Treats was one of those highly designed pop-up shops a normal person might notice on the cover of an expensive magazine while waiting to pay for a tomato, some orzo, and olive oil at Whole Foods. What kind of women bought those magazines? Probably straight white women prior to picking up their children from private school; women who slummed at Whole Foods, not women like her, who usually shopped for groceries at Walmart. She biked to work not because it was better for the planet, but because it was cheaper than taking the bus.

And because it was better for the planet. That too.

This suddenly appearing new bakery had a black marble façade with pink and green detailing. Parquet floors. High-ceilinged with a sparkling green chandelier over the entry that looked like it was made of crystallized vines. Not the sort of place Helen could possibly afford, but today was a special day. Today was her 35th birthday.

She made an impulsive decision: She would buy herself a muffin if they looked good, no matter the price, because she deserved a treat.

She kicked the bike up the granite path, and it flew towards the door of the shop as if drawn by powerful forces. She wrenched the handlebars to the left and the bike whined and creaked beneath her.

"Stupid bike," she muttered, and her front wheel wobbled as if she'd hurt its feelings. She dismounted and apologized to the thing, then felt ridiculous. Her whole life seemed to revolve around making apologies these days. She needed a spine. She resolved to be more forceful. To take what she wanted.

Immediately her actions belied her wishes again: She locked her bike against a support column, meekly wondering if the sign forbidding parking applied to bikes. The last thing she needed was to have her bike impounded. When Helen pushed the glass door open, the scent of vanilla, cloves, and sugar nearly buckled her knees. Being watchful of every penny meant frequent hunger. Her stomach growled, and she shifted her messenger bag so that the water sloshing inside the bottle would cover the pitiful sound of her belly.

A thoughtful woman in worn jeans and work boots was the only other customer in the store. This woman chewed at an unpainted lip, seemed unable to decide between blueberry lemon and banana clove. Helen couldn't breathe looking at her. Torn-off sleeves framing sculpted biceps; an indifferent toss of short hair.

"Go on ahead." The stranger waved Helen forward. Her voice was husky, a werewolf voice, full of repressed anger and growls. Helen wondered if this woman was the sort to have chosen a spirit animal or if she had outgrown mysticism or was woke to cultural appropriation. Helen wanted to know her better. She wished with all her might that this woman might speak to her. The meeting felt like a gift, and Helen thanked the woman with perhaps too much breath in her tone. She got an arched eyebrow in response.

"No need to thank me," the woman said with a shrug. "My shift doesn't start for another hour. It's my 35th birthday, and I thought I'd treat myself."

The coincidence gave Helen a jolt. "Wow. Happy birthday," she said, completely flummoxed. It was another gift, an opening for conversation; she really ought to tell the woman they'd been born on the same day. Helen wasn't dating anyone, and this woman had an interested glint in her eye. Helen didn't see a ring. The look was right. Possible anyway. But Helen's voice failed her. She noted the woman's piercing: an owl stud with tiny emerald eyes. Athena's symbol. Wisdom. Helen was not obviously gay, and assumed this woman, like most women that were her type, would overlook her. Helen was small and Asian, but she wouldn't conform for the fetishists. The women she liked always desired a gorgeous intellectual with straight hair and red lips. In college, Helen had gone through that phase (hair flat-ironed, Superman glasses) but dropped it when she dropped out to work full-time—the community college was expensive, and its education wasn't worth the debt she was incurring. She got more out of watching webinars on YouTube.

They shared a wry smile and the stranger looked interested when Helen pointed to the blueberry and identified the combo of blueberry lemon as her favorite.

"That'll be $23.79," the elderly cashier muttered. The price seemed to be no surprise to the other customer, but Helen's mouth went dry.

"Twenty-three…?"

"Twenty-three seventy-nine," the cashier repeated in an impatient crone's voice. In addition to heavy black eyeliner, the elderly woman wore a black scarf in a knot to hide her throat, and it reminded Helen of an ancient stewardess she'd once seen in an old movie. A scary movie where untying the knot had horrifying consequences. The old woman ran a knobby finger down her bristly chin. "You want what you deserve or not?"

Helen didn't want to seem cheap. The other customer smiled and tilted her head, waiting. Was this normal? Did regular people pay more than twenty dollars for bakery products? It had been such a long time since she had treated herself. In fact, it had been several years since she had walked into a store that lacked huge shopping carts. She was always so careful. So frugal. Haunted by her first and last girlfriend, who had ended their tempestuous eight-year relationship by cleaning out the bank account, and selling all the jewelry and art they had bought together as investments for their future. ("I hate the term retirement account," Bonnie had said in that flip way that Helen couldn't resist. "Let's just buy nice things and sell them later when-and-if we need the money.") Bonnie had relocated to Baja with the sleek bank teller who had helped her pull the scam. That had been years ago, but Helen could still hear echoes of the reprimands and cautions of her disapproving father, her tight-lipped mother, both warning her against Bonnie, both horrified their only daughter was gay. Both dead now, still believing the whole situation was a well-deserved penance for her lifestyle. Why was she still ruled by their criticism? She had bounced back financially if not emotionally. Her student loans had been paid off. She owned her small home outright. She took in an old rescue dog named Pumpkin. She even had dreams of traveling to Costa Rica to see monkeys in the wild, of selling her modest one-bedroom house and buying something on a lake where her Labrador could run free and swim. She was building up savings for these things, and for retirement, for the happily-ever-after that she deserved, the one Bonnie had stolen from her. A flash startled her out of her reverie. She staggered a step to the side and grabbed the cold marble countertop for balance. What was that?

She blinked in the ordinary light of the shop. Shook her head to clear it. The cashier was staring at her.

"Well?" The old woman jerked her chin to the display. Her black buttons strained against her fleshy torso.

When was she planning to start living this life she was saving for? She was thirty-five today. Twenty bucks for a muffin. Was this how other women lived? She had once overheard a coworker sighing that she regularly spent $600 coloring her hair. To keep her own hair properly dark, Helen used a box that cost far less than this muffin, and was considering just letting herself go gray. Was she missing out?

"No, it's fine," Helen stammered, "That is, yes. I do. I want it."

Her heart raced. The other woman's eyes lingered on the display, Helen's legs, and Helen's face, as if assessing her anew. She hummed under her breath, as if discovering some interesting bone at an archaeological dig.

The cashier's gnarled hands bore a large ruby ring on the

left index finger and wrapped the blueberry lemon muffin in delicate tissue, twisting the top of the tissue into the shape of a heart, then placed the treat into a waxy white bag as carefully as if it were a live animal. Helen kept her face calm and switched from cash to credit card.

The other customer stared at the muffin display, biting her pinky nail in a vulnerable way that made Helen's heart hurt. Late for work and overwhelmed by self-loathing, Helen's hands refused to work the lock, and she was still at her bike when the other woman emerged.

"I got the same thing you did," the woman said. "Need a ride anywhere?"

"No thanks," Helen replied, extricating a piece of hair from her mouth where the sudden breeze had flicked it.

"Oh, okay then," said the woman. There was a pause as she stood there, holding the pretty waxy bag that matched Helen's. "Well, okay."

"Okay," Helen said, and the bike lock clattered to the pavement, startling both of them. Their nervous laughter mingled.

"Bikes," the woman said. "Great exercise."

"I'm late for work," Helen said, straddling the bike, without revealing that they shared a birthday.

"I could give you a lift."

"I need to work off the muffin."

Helen rode hard and fast, forcing her lungs to burn in punishment of her timidity. Kicking up gravel in the hopes that she might wipe out and hurt herself. Another missed opportunity in a string of blank calendar days.

She arrived at work early. Punishment enough.

***

To ameliorate the exorbitant price of the muffin, she decided to have it as her lunch. The morning passed slowly. No one spoke to her, which was normal. She sorted claims and called clients to discuss their policies. Some of them hung up on her. Sometimes she told them it was her birthday and got a surprised, "Oh. Happy birthday," to which she replied with gratitude. She was fully aware that her life was empty. Her dog was sixteen years old and could barely make it in and out of the apartment. Helen did charitable work in order to have reasons to speak to other people: walked the AIDS walk, biked for breast cancer…there were few diseases or causes she had not supported. She had three personal social media accounts and posted occasional likes and comments on high school friends' family vacations and travels on each platform. What else should she be doing? Should one join a church or a temple, just to find companionship? That seemed wrong. She opened Facebook and wrote a quick line about buying a $23 muffin at Wild Witch Treats. Jason Womicki liked the comment. No one else reacted. Twenty of her fifty-two Facebook friends had already posted "Happy Birthday Helen" messages, three with blinking cakes, but not one had offered to meet her for coffee or take her out to lunch. None of her coworkers were Facebook friends. The office remained its usual bleak, fluorescent-lit wasteland.

The muffin waited for her in the break room. Her thoughts, like tentative turkey vultures, kept circling around to the muffin. It was extraordinary, to pay so much for a pastry.

She found a half-burnt candle in the detritus of a drawer where the coffee filters were kept and palmed it quickly, so Harry from Accounting wouldn't see. He was making a cappuccino. Helen smelled the unmistakable tang of burning wires from the back of the machine. She might have mentioned something, but instead she joined Harry in listening to Sandy, who was bragging—again—about how she worked out both before and after work.

"Say, Helen, do *you* work out?" the heavily tattooed receptionist said in that strong Virginia drawl. An unlit cigarette dangled from Sandy's mouth. Helen had never actually seen the young woman smoke; Sandy was a health-buff with a perfect body. Helen also suspected that Sandy's Southern accent was assumed—for four years now, the receptionist had kept explaining that she was only temporary, that she was really an actress, that she was just waiting for the right role. Helen thought maybe Sandy's entire story was fake, including the accent. Of course no one could smoke anywhere near the office, so it was hard to prove anything. And she wasn't sure if it would have changed anything to know for certain if Sandy had ever been out on an audition. She was the most coveted, most popular girl in the office; did truth have anything to do with that?

Sandy had gotten tired of waiting for Helen to reply. "I guess even if you did work out, no one would notice, huh?"

Helen shrugged and Harry turned swiftly from her

presumably to check up on his cappuccino, though Helen could tell he was trying to hide laughter. Sandy sashayed out of the lunchroom, then ducked back in.

"Hey, Helen, five of us girls are going out for lunch, what do you think?" Sandy left a dramatic pause long enough for Helen to hope she was being invited to join them, "Can you cover my phones, sweetie? You're not doing anything, right?"

Helen turned back to the fridge. Nodded. Sandy laughed and pounded the wall with the flat of her hand.

"Good girl. Knew you would. Thanks a mil."

If only they would all just leave. Sandy gathered up co-workers while Helen took her bakery bag from the communal refrigerator. She ran her fingers over the pretty gold seal. "Wild Witch Treats," she whispered, and her skin erupted with the same inexplicable tingles she'd felt that morning upon first discovering the bakery. Twenty-three dollars for a blueberry muffin was a lot. She had to keep reminding herself it was her birthday. Her birthday. She was one year older. One year more experienced. This was her day. Hers.

She brought the bag to the front desk where Sandy usually sat. The phone was ringing. The bakery's golden seal seemed to glow. It made her eyes hurt.

"Apex Auto Insurance," she said into the headset. "May I help you?" As she dealt with the customer, she unfolded a tissue and used it to soften the white-blue glare of Sandy's desk lamp. Helen was good at her job and had actual work to do. She rolled Sandy's chair over, and reached for the stack of unsorted hardcopy claims on her own desk.

"I'm very glad I could help you, sir. Have a nice day." She dropped the huge stack of claims on Sandy's desk. The headset chafed. She adjusted it so it was no longer Sandy-sized.

The gabbling group of happy women emerged from the break room, having absorbed Harry into their party. The talking stopped when they saw Helen working on claims as well as answering their phone calls.

"You're so reliable, Helen," Sandy cooed, grabbing a vibrant purple scarf from the back of her chair and a pair of designer flats from her lowest drawer, "You're a doll. We won't be more than an hour, two hours tops. It's just so lucky that we picked a quiet day."

Helen waited until they were gone.

"It's my birthday," she whispered to the empty office.

The phone rang again and she adjusted the headset so she could talk while breaking the seal on the waxy white bag. A sound like the celebratory popping of a cork surprised her and she fumbled for words with the client on the phone as the longer tendrils of her hair tugged towards the opening. It was as if the bag contained a strong vacuum. She also smelled smoke, and for a moment she thought it was coming from the break room, but then she thought maybe it was coming from the bag.

"I'm so sorry, Mr. Mihimoto," Helen interrupted. "I'm going to have to place you on a rather long hold. Unless you'd rather call back later?" As she rather expected, the guy cursed at her and hung up.

"Wild Witch Treats," she said, this time to test the effect and indeed, her skin tingled head to toe and the wind sucking her hair towards the bag increased. Now she could distinctly hear a fire crackling from inside the bag. It was disconcerting, but what a great marketing trick. Totally worth twenty bucks. She looked inside and was only mildly disappointed to find just the muffin.

She pulled it out. Crumbly, yellow, with enormous blueberries, the muffin looked rich and moist, certainly the most perfect muffin she had ever seen. She was surrounded in a cloud of lemon and blueberry scent. She wiped the end of the used candle with a tissue then stuck it into the center of the little cake. The overhead lights brightened for a second.

Feeling slightly unnerved, she waited, but nothing else changed. She lit the candle with one of Sandy's extra lighters.

This was certainly the most depressing birthday party Helen had ever had. No balloons. No streamers. Not even the birthday song. Still, as her mother always said, *It's your life. Only you can turn it around.* Rising from the chair to ensure she was alone, she spread her arms wide as a little girl twirling on a lawn and sang *Happy Birthday to Me.*

And well, why not, she added the hot girl from the bakery.

Happy birthday, dear me & bakery-girl, happy birthday to us!

Wax dripped onto the muffin's perfect crust as the candle burned down. She whispered her wish into the emptiness and blew.

The candle did not go out. It exploded. Helen was thrown against the back wall of the reception area. Sparks flew onto the carefully sorted piles of paperwork on her desk and set it all aflame. The blaze spread rapidly, despite Helen's efforts to put it out. The sprinklers came on, but the still flames spread.

By the time the girls (and Harry) returned from lunch, Helen stood on a pile of wet plastics, covered in soot. Her bicycle's front wheel had been mangled by a firefighter from Engine 6 who needed to get to the window the bike rack was blocking.

Long before learning that no one had been hurt, without even acknowledging Helen's near-death experience, Sandy had taken one look at the smoldering building and launched into a string of wailing vowels that started somewhere in the middle of a drawled-out "oh my dear Lord Jesus" and ended in crocodile tears over the expensive audition-outfit she'd left in her desk that was probably ruined and how that would wreck her chances for pilot season. Her sycophants surrounded her to pat her back and shoulders, overlooking Helen's ruined bike and sodden shoes. To keep Sandy from hyperventilating, Harry handed the buff bottle-blonde a lit cigarette. Sandy reached out an inked arm, inhaled deeply with half-lidded eyes, and began to cough so violently that Harry backed away. Between coughs, Sandy loudly blamed the steaming rubble for her fit, but everyone had noticed that her voice had suddenly lost its Dixie. The four women and Harry stood in a half-ring, dazed, the enchantment broken.

Helen grinned, but not because Sandy had been exposed as a fraud.

In her pocket, she had the phone number of that firefighter from Engine 6, a burly woman who wore an owl in her eyebrow. Turned out, they happened to share a birthday and a love of blueberry lemon treats, and since she had mangled the wheel of Helen's bike, Susan (for that was the firefighter's name) was delighted to offer her a ride home after work, and then some.

Empty

Her phone vibrates with yet another text message from her boss's assistant, Fran.

On his desk by 3:30 or you're out.

Sarah grimaces, types one word—soon—but the message won't send. Stupid iPhone. To keep her mind on her impending commission check, she presses the reset button on the printer for the fifteenth time in as many minutes. The printer reboots and—despite her held breath, curses, and prayers—its red alarm light flashes.

"You are not out of paper!" she shouts at the machine. (Her shout is at office volume: under her breath, but with the vituperation of a sailor who discovers he's on the wrong ship.) Self-doubt comes next: she opens the flimsy plastic drawer. Full. To the brim. A pillow of white 20lb bond. A princess could sleep on it.

"*Come on!*"

She's no princess; she works for a cheap realtor near a strip of car dealerships. Her nicest clothes are from Target, and even so, she's drowning. Around here, everything is going out of business. Vanishing. She presses the reset button again. The printer reboots and—the red alarm light flashes.

Instead of cursing, she does the hand exercises her father once taught her. He repaired rotary phones back when that was a career and not a joke. She fans the fingers of both hands into bony starfish, as if rigidity itself could solve the printer problem. Clenches them into fists. Fans them. Clenches. Her teeth hurt.

How do you fight the machines? You can't.

Her father's stress-relieving exercises aren't helping.

So.

She e-mails the document to Fran with instructions to print it. The pressure lifts from her shoulders and neck, and she floats like a fat Macy's balloon caught dangerously, ecstatically by the wind. She wants to high-five someone. Looks around. Blinks.

Where is everyone? Lunch? A meeting to which she hasn't been invited? Not one of the cubicles is occupied.

Steady now—she ducks into the break room. Light pours through the window, but even the dust motes are still. Outside, another dealership has closed its doors.

Where's the party?

Coffee, black; she'll be herself again. Who has she become? Her raw-bitten nails are not what she'd expected. She remembers preteen hours spent painting them with polishes from palest pink to scarlet, all shades stolen from her mother's vanity. She remembers wanting to be pretty, to be married, to belong to someone. Dreaming of awards, of recognition. Offspring. Her real life is a monthly battle with incoming messages (an intractable enemy) and the automated phone calls of credit agencies claiming to represent her best interests before putting her on hold. If only she could win the war with her past. Once, she'd bought new shoes believing they would change her life. Now she only wants to pay her bills, to have sex on occasion, and to update her status on Facebook more than once a season.

That; plus a cup of coffee.

Impossibly, the Keurig is also obdurate: nothing is brewed or brewing. She jiggles the plug. Checks water level: full. The grounds: dark, dry, and waiting. Frustrated, she twists her mug so its message of hope faces the plain kitchen wall, and opens the drawer where she, Dolores, and Trevor hide high-calorie snacks.

Empty.

She looks out into the deserted room of cubicles and scribbles a yellow sticky note: *Those were mine. Please never eat the last Pop-Tart.*

She crosses out *please*.

Sticks the note inside the drawer and slams it shut. A cloud of dust wafts over her. She sneezes and can't find a box of Kleenex. Uses a disposable napkin from a Chinese food place. The tiny square seems to be made of something less durable than tissue yet manages to feel as abrasive as plastic.

Opens the mini fridge: just mustard packets, sour skim milk, and a jar holding two grape jelly globules like bottom feeders in a fish tank. Nothing else. Not that she'd really had hopes of an eggroll.

There's a thought.

Fresh air. Takeout from the Chinese place down the street.

Maybe she can meet up with her current boyfriend, Matt, a technician for Dell on the second floor. Maybe he'll pick up the tab since she doesn't get paid until Friday; she hates to put something as lame as eggrolls on her credit card. Before calling, she goes to her laptop to pre-plan a message so she doesn't say something dumb. She's only been out with Matt twice, met him during a building-wide safety seminar. She isn't planning a picket fence, but hopes to see him for a few more pseudo-romantic nights. Decides to end with "call me" in the brightest voice she can manage. Her laptop flashes an alert: system offline. Her e-mail, with its urgent attachment, is still unsent.

When she scoops up her iPhone to call Fran, the display flashes a sleek red battery symbol and winks out.

Her stomach rumbles, overwhelming her disbelief.

She clicks the e-mail attachment: Unable to find file.

Her cheap suit is stifling. Sweat trickles down her back. She needs people or food—immediately. She leaves the office, pockets her card key. Greets Alan Mills in the long corridor, but the realtor doesn't respond; just walks on by, texting someone on his Android.

She enters the elevator alone and presses the L for Lobby. The round button doesn't light; instead the bell-alarm goes off so loud her teeth ache. The doors close in front of her face, shutting out everything she has ever known. The elevator descends. The overhead lights wink out; the alarm batters the darkness. She covers her ears, but the noise and the falling never stop.

Cineplex

When people ask, I say that I'm a physicist who serves on the board of a nonprofit science research agency headquartered in New York. This is true, basically. My area of expertise is parallel universes. At any given moment, I know all the things that ever did or might happen in a given location. For example, I travel to a small town in Texas; College Station, say, which is one of those crazy towns that sprang up in the middle of nowhere surrounding a university and then turned into a cultural center for people who appreciate landscape watercolors and classical or country music. I sit there at the corner of Farm Road 2818 and Wellborne Road in a rental car, some six-cylinder piece of crap with lousy shocks, and instead of four lanes of asphalt, black as burnt bodies, stretching to each corner of the compass, I see two dirt roads intersecting with a flashing red light above them. I see a 1965 station wagon with wooden sides approaching this intersection at the same time as a 1968 black-top Chevelle with whitewall tires, and then, while the lady behind the wheel of the Acura waves to me that my light has turned green, I watch the Chevelle blow through the stop sign and hear the crunch of metal as it rams into the front of the station wagon. All six of the passengers involved—two in the Chevy and four in the station wagon, three kids and their harried mom—are instantly killed. The lady in the Acura honks her horn and finally passes me and yells something at me out the window, and the last thing I see of her is a bumper sticker that proclaims her stand on abortion.

 I'll give you another example. I'm awkwardly shopping at a sale in Tribeca, a swanky neighborhood in Manhattan, in a cute kids' boutique crammed full of mommies and fancy strollers. They don't like a man in their space, nor how clueless I am about these toys, but I'm finding items I've never seen anywhere else, really cool things that actually make me excited enough to want to buy them: soft androgynous dolls with curving smiles and mismatched eyes, racers from Japan powered by ghosts, sea monkey space stations. I reach for a bubble gun shaped like a lollypop and my eyes unfocus just enough to show an empty lot. I'm standing beside a drugged-out teenager who has fallen to her knees and is reaching up toward the sky, begging for forgiveness. It hits so fast I can't tell if I'm seeing past or future, just this girl who is high enough not to feel the broken glass embedding itself into her knees. She is screaming and someone from an upper tenement floor throws a flowerpot at her. It flies past and shatters with great force, and she breaks down sobbing, alternating between prayers of thanks that it missed her and admonitions that it should have killed her. How can I shop? I have to leave the store, disappointing the single mom who owns it, depriving her daughter of the Wii game she was going to get that weekend. Making all the other women in the store sneer at me and sigh something about shopping being left to the female gender.

***

It's depressing, being a demigod. It's not just the places that waver in and out of existence; you can't rely on the people either, and because I'm only half, these abilities come and go—but when they come, wow. I can see everything a person ever experienced, and multiple courses their lives might take. Last year, for example, in California, I shook hands with this lovely executive. Frizzy red hair, golden smile, a suit she'd bought while on holiday in Paris with her husband, and I knew in an instant that she was ten weeks pregnant, she'd lost her first baby at twenty-five weeks, and the one growing right now was either going to suffer crippling asthma her entire life or be shot in a convenience store robbery at age twenty. I also knew that the executive's husband was having an affair and that she hadn't yet found out. Her aging mother wasn't telling her that she had cancer because she didn't want her to worry. Her sister was making three times her salary. Her boss was going to offer her a fantastic raise, but she would turn it down to stay home with Olivia. If events went the way of the asthma, she would cut her hair short and gain forty-five pounds, but her marriage would recover from the affair and they would have a second child named Samuel, who would be a rather successful entrepreneur, selling his services as a

YouTube film director. If events went the way of the convenience store, she would break it off with her husband, become a director of the PR firm that was hosting this event, leave, and form a wildly successful breakout business with her sister. And when her daughter was shot, she would take sleeping pills to join the girl.

I could alter all this, quite easily. I could drift over to the timeline where her husband had changed his mind about the affair. In that timeline, she hadn't lost the first child.

On the other hand, I had instigated the conversation to hit her up for a donation for nonprofit research, a donation she would willingly give—and in the timeline with the living child, she wasn't rich enough to bother.

Meanwhile, I was holding a blue martini, expected to make small talk. I gestured toward the glossy heads of the glamorous group assembled in the Hollywood loft.

"Lovely party," I said.

"I'm so glad you came," she replied, her hand on her Pilates-flat belly.

I pointed to the gesture, raised an eyebrow. Half her mouth smiled while her eyes widened. The expression made me want to laugh because she'd first used it when she was six, caught by her mother drawing hearts on the floor with a crayon.

"Is it so obvious?" She giggled. "I'm not telling anyone yet. Shh!"

Okay and sometimes it's fun: to enter a house and feel a father's first few moments home, linger in the joy of his kids leaping on him in gratitude and happiness at his existence; to walk a beach, privy to dozens of sandy moonlit trysts and skinny-dipped wedding proposals. I can use my knowledge to eliminate the fear an old woman feels waiting for a flu shot by asking about her long-dead sister who used to hold her hand at the doctor. When the ability manifests most strongly, I can read what has and will happen, and I can use this knowledge for good—to guide, yes, but often just to distract and entertain.

Not enough credit is given to things that distract and entertain.

But as much as I love my immortal life, it isn't easy to be a demigod—you have to practice all the time; it's draining. Still, I suppose that's better than the alternative. For me, being out of practice feels like being an ex–concert pianist whose fingers twitch whenever he hears a fifteen-year-old throw down Rachmaninoff's Third Concerto. Ever been late and had a train pull out of the station, almost as if it were mocking you? I was probably in the vicinity and off my game. Sorry. It's a real calling, godhood, and unless you're willing to devote yourself to your talents one hundred percent, well, it's best left to others who are more dedicated.

That's what I tell myself when I'm down—then I pick up the pieces and forge ahead.

Even though I'm only a demigod, I take my responsibilities seriously.

***

Still, there comes a time in every artist's life when he questions his path.

Mine began with an event—an overwhelming one. Which

is saying a lot. By now, I have become rather used to having four or five alternate realities layer themselves upon the current time and place. I peel past and future like an onion, and just like an onion they can make me cry.

But now? I feel like an idiot—and no one likes to feel that way, least of all a god. Anyway, I've been gearing up to propose to my girlfriend. She isn't immortal. In fact, she isn't unusual in any way, really. I am desperately in love with her, perhaps because of her very ordinary and simple life. No tragedies have marred her psyche, other than the usual pet hamsters dying within days of each other, small high school heartbreaks including a minor betrayal by a best friend and one piece of nastiness involving a boyfriend who came weeping out of the closet during their prom date. In general, her life has been lovely. She's from a small town in Texas (if you must know, it is, indeed, College Station). She attends church weekly, though she isn't obsessed by missionary work or anything else a non-Christian could find offensive. She loves her aging parents and visits them for a monthly family game night—her sisters drive down too and all of them play *Life* or *Monopoly* or *Boggle* or whatever they all agree upon. They are happy.

She is happy.

Her name is Tracey, and she wants children. That was my first sign that things might eventually go awry. In every future possibility this world offers, none of my offspring are ever going to amount to anything much. Okay, maybe they won't become axe-murderers, but the oldest son will be a plumber, the next one an accountant, the girl some sort of painter-slash-waitress—

and this sort of everyday job isn't something that I can get my brain around. I am a young demigod, after all. I have high expectations. How can I father a girl who will live in permanent credit card debt, tied to her mother's occasional bailouts until Tracey dies from a rare blood infection and leaves her daughter a third of everything, and even then the girl will keep going out with ridiculous boyfriends who dump her and make her cry? I ask you, would you doom your own offspring to a fate like that?

I want my kids to shape the world, and if they're just going to be ordinary, then honestly, why even bother? Tracey and I can have a great time (this is another possibility I have seen) traveling the world, experiencing new foods, watching sunsets over various oceans. Why introduce children into such a blissful picture?

Tracey is a preschool teacher. Dark hair falls down her back like a magician's curtain hiding something soft and living that you want to touch. She has brown eyes with little emerald flecks that brighten when she laughs or cries. Cute glasses that change with the seasons. A smile that flashes in and out of existence like the Don't Walk signals that make everyone in New York City step up their pace. The kids in her class love her and throw their arms around her the second their mothers turn their backs. Tracey loves them too and treats each one like a miniature adult, asking about their day and listening with genuine interest to the contents of their lunch boxes.

I am, for a fact, in love. Not easy for a god—but as you've probably guessed, my mother was human. It was one of those blah-blah-blah mythic events, you know. The swan? The bull?

That sort of thing. My dad, she said, was a beautiful truck driver she never saw again. I've spoken to him—he dropped in on my twelfth birthday to meet me, and he really was beautiful. I could see the ever-present sparkly shimmer that to mortals just seems like charisma. As with all meetings like this, I probably learned more about him than he did about me. Not the least was that he'd seduced my mortal mother only because she'd reminded him of a certain star of the silver screen.

On the other hand, he, being a full-on god, likely knew everything about me the second we sat down across from each other at the diner that had once belonged to a Greek immigrant whose wife was killed in a political skirmish in the old country. That diner would be destroyed three years from the date of our lunch to make room for a boutique hotel, but the economy would not recover enough to fill it, so the lot would grow over in weeds, and a family of rabbits would take up residence, prompting a local schoolteacher to campaign to turn the space into a public garden … you see how hard it can be to concentrate on anything when you've got these abilities. Meeting my dad was an event that blended in with the rest of the events that had or would happen in that diner, neither more important nor less. When our meeting was over, all I really knew about him was what the human side of me could infer. I could tell he had never truly loved my mother. I could tell he was vaguely proud of me but equally ashamed that I even existed. I could tell he hoped I wouldn't want to see him again.

You can't live simply when you're part god. You just can't.

Getting back to the story. As part of gearing up to propose to

Tracey, I had to, of course, buy an engagement ring. Where else to do this but the Diamond District in New York? I was going to be there anyway. My annual board meeting was coming up (in addition to the science nonprofit, I'm also on the board of directors for one of the big firms responsible for that city "going green"—sorry I can't disclose which one, but if you Google my name and "Treasurer" it comes right up). Anyway, I was in New York, messing around with minor events as I often did, just for kicks. I'd gotten the plane there early, chose a timeline that made the taxi sail through traffic from JFK, checked in to the hotel and got my room upgraded by remarking on the desk matron's past as a model and complimenting her luscious eyes. And I found myself with a three-hour cushion of time before the appointment I'd made with the jeweler on Forty-Seventh Street.

So I did what lots of people do to kill time—I went to a movie. There's a big Cineplex on Forty-Second Street, several stories high, with twenty-some movies to choose from. I like movies because they are created and finished—no parallel timelines to dive into; those are all on the cutting room floor of some studio back in Hollywood.

So in I went, ready to be distracted and entertained.

The theater my movie was playing in, Theater Six, held visions too dreadful to bear. It was a bad place. Another god controlled it. If the movie hadn't been the only one worth the price of admission, I would have changed theaters rather than spend time in that place, but instead, I blocked out the violence as best as I could and focused my entire attention on the screen.

The movie I'd selected was a painful, mind-blowing art

film, and when the lights rose after 124 minutes plus trailers, I was rubbing the hope out of my eyes, wishing that genius were rewarded, wishing that beauty were better appreciated, that sort of thing. I stood up and felt dozens of spider-webs tear. I ignored the strippers who would (or wouldn't) have sex with clients to feed their heroin habits, though they gyrated wherever the folded theater seats allowed. I ignored the layers and layers of men whose lives had been ruined by a desire for the perfect fantasy in the sex club that had been at this spot before Mayor Giuliani's attempt to Disney-fy the city by transforming Forty-Second Street into a family-friendly tourist center, and I tried to concentrate on the empty theater seats. Even in Manhattan, few people go to the movies in the morning. Any humans I saw were likely to be ghosts or glimpses of things yet to come.

There was one patron, however. Near the exit. An old woman dressed in a suit that had seen better days. She carried a thick leather bag that seemed a bit too heavy for her. She too was wiping tears from her eyes.

"Good movie," I said.

She laughed as if I'd been wearing a clown nose. I thought I'd just keep walking, but she reached out and grabbed my arm.

"I want to tell you," she said. "I have to tell someone, and you seem like the right sort of person. I'll buy you a coffee if you just sit and talk with me."

But I, of course, already knew. I had known from the moment I walked into that theater. Before even meeting her.

"I'll buy the coffee," I told her. What could I do? Even full gods can walk away, but it does tarnish the reputation, and after a while you're evil, plain and simple. Doing nothing is as bad as doing the wrong thing, sometimes. "We'll go to the coffee shop upstairs. I think it opened at eleven."

"That's right," she said, and from her expression I wondered if she knew my history as well as I could see hers. I didn't offer to carry her bag, and she seemed grateful for that kindness. I followed her as she shuffled up the slowly ramping aisle. I reached over her snowy head to help her with the door, and her breath caught as if she could see the little sparkles that my movements cast for those with the right eyesight.

"Ladies first," I said. She shrugged, and for a second she was still the beautiful actress she'd been in the 1950s.

We took the elevator to two. She ordered a latte with skim milk. I got my usual double espresso. I spent some time rubbing the rim of my cup with the lemon rind before I dropped the sliver of peel into the demitasse. She stared at me through the steam rising from her bowl. A stripper screamed in the background, but the bouncer was quick and pulled the guy with the knife out of the room. The city kids holding hands with their guardians squealed over a shipment of carrot seed. The old lady didn't flinch. She closed her eyes to better smell the coffee.

"Not often I get to indulge," she murmured.

Her daily routine sent the espresso straight to my blood. She lived here, she told me in a whisper. In the Cineplex. She went to the ATM, withdrew twenty dollars, bought a nine-dollar senior ticket, and slept through one movie after another until well after dark; then she'd change into the ridiculous silver sequined dress in her bag, throw on huge dark sunglasses, and head for the clubs.

The bouncers always let her in; Miss Charlotte was a fixture. She'd been a starlet in the 1950s, had slumped in the '60s and '70s, had emerged from an ugly prescription drug habit completely clean and shockingly healthy, had blown out sixty-five candles to become an official senior citizen, and the less makeup she wore, the more beautiful people thought she was. Suddenly her love of big hats, sparkles, and large gaudy jewelry was charming and quaint, rather than pathetic and creepy. The more she aged, the cuter the club kids thought she was—and as they themselves aged out, she aged back in. Now she was known at all the velvet ropes and was eagerly welcomed as a local character, the only Truman Capote left in the city. But the starlet had never been on the books long enough to receive Social Security, and she was too proud to apply for general assistance. Even in the glory days, her penthouse had always been far beyond her means, and eventually she'd received one eviction notice too many.

***

Despite her cine-motel lifestyle, she watched her six-digit savings drop slowly to five and now four. She kept a tiny storage facility in upper Harlem, where she went every day at 8:00 a.m. to change clothes, soak her dentures, and pack a change of clothes into her leather bag. Winters were harsh, but the Cineplex was warm. She ate what people gave her, an early morning dinner of popcorn and nachos when she could find them abandoned in the seats before nodding off. Nights she ate better: most of the clubs had free appetizers, and in a pinch, the bartenders always let her eat their olives and oranges. Sometimes the olives were stuffed with almonds or little pearl onions. Some of the fancier places had lychees and wasabi peas. She had been living like this for almost fifteen years.

"I want to tell someone what I saw," she said. "I've been afraid they'd find out how I live if I went to the police."

As if to give her time to reconsider, the server broke in to ask if we wanted food. I ordered raisin scones for both of us. Miss Charlotte beamed at me.

"My favorite," she cooed. "You certainly are a gentleman. Your mother raised you right."

Again I wondered if she knew more than she let on, but nothing in her past or future seemed to suggest she was anything but what she appeared to be: an old lady down on her luck, using her wits to get by, suffering under the guilt of an unreported crime. My mother had struggled with me—I was a chore, as you can imagine, always knowing what the teachers were going to say, knowing just what would drive them to screaming fits, or worse, to tears. I didn't see the point of making friends with people who were going to die in forty years, or worse, in five. My mother stood by me through it all. She knew what she had done in bringing me into the world. Lucky for me, I looked like her—I couldn't have had such an ordinary life if I'd inherited my father's jet-black eyes, his white shock of hair, or his massive arms. It was bad enough I was this tall, but some people are. Even some people who aren't demigods. Look at the Lakers.

"I should have brought him to justice, but, well, I didn't know what I had seen. That is, I knew I'd seen a horrible event, but I wasn't sure they'd ever catch the man, and the girl, she was already dead."

He'd twisted his girlfriend's neck. I had seen it as I sank into my seat ready for the movie to begin. I heard the snap again as she remembered it, saw the man's eyes grow horrified, then cold. Felt the trickle of Miss Charlotte's sweat as she ducked her head back down behind the seats.

"I'd fallen asleep, see. I was watching this movie and just, well, when you get old, sleep comes when it wants." Her eyes searched me for doubt. I kept my face neutral and attentive. "I woke up when he started yelling at her. He thought they were alone, see. Kept asking her to have sex with him. Said that no one ran the projectors anymore, just computers. She said no. Felt someone was watching. Jesus or someone. He slapped her for bringing Jesus into it. Said it was blasphemy. They were a wreck, those two. But when the fighting just got worse, I finally poked my head up, thinking if he saw me, he'd stop it with the slaps. She was crying, sure, but she was also calling him unbelievably foul names, calling his entire life into question."

She looked into her coffee cup. "There's no good way for a woman to defend herself, is there? Not if she loves the guy."

Because of course she too had allowed her producer to smack her around; she'd hoped she could change him, hoped he wasn't as serious about the other girls, hoped the promises he kept feeding her were truth. She'd had no choice but to believe in him: by then her entire image was tied up in her films.

People never think they have a choice.

"I saw him grab her face and I thought he was going to kiss

her; it was so gentle the way he laid his hands on her, and then …" She shuddered, and like her I had to endure the memory of that snap, like a rake handle breaking in two. "I ducked and he ran. I knew from the way she was slumped over two seats that she was dead. I never even checked. He ran, and I ran too. Five minutes after he left, I went to the bathroom, was sick there if you really want to know. Sick because I didn't know what to do. Didn't know if I should stay to talk with the police or sneak into yet another theater and hide. They wouldn't find her body for an hour yet; the movie they'd been watching wasn't half done. I could even leave the theater altogether, that's what I realized. And in the end, that's what I did. Walked right out into the snow."

Her eyes welled up and she wiped her tears away with a much-used tissue she'd pulled from a sleeve. "I can't believe I still come here. So many ghosts."

"Which theater was it?" I asked, though I knew, because I had seen it. Six. That end of the Cineplex shook with violence. Not just the murder Miss Charlotte had witnessed, but the call girl years before, and the heroin overdoses, and the child who years from now would be taken there by the sex offender who would opt for a death by cop in public rather than be brought in for questioning.

"You were there. Didn't you feel it?"

"I read about that murder in the papers," I lied. "I followed it. Did you?"

"No," she admitted. "I saw the headlines but I couldn't bring myself to look any farther. I was too afraid the police would make a public appeal for witnesses. I couldn't have stayed away then."

Inside her bag was her sparkly silver dress with flapper fringe in Size 2. Silver shoes with two-inch heels. A top hat with three bedraggled ostrich feathers on a sequined band. She was an icon on the club scene, an inspiration to the pretty and empty heads who couldn't conceive of her years of hardship. Who couldn't imagine that she was there only because she had nowhere else to go. To them, she was a role model. To them, she was a hero. When-I-grow-up-I-hope-to-be-Miss-Charlotte. Surrogate grandma. Glamorous great-aunt.

A lie tingled on the tip of my tongue. All I had to do was utter it. I could make it true. It would be easy.

They caught the guy, was all I had to say. *The police found him because the girl had left a journal. He went to jail for life. Died there, in fact.*

I could make it true.

In that universe, Miss Charlotte's scone would stop halfway to her lips, forgotten. Her forehead would relax. Lips quiver.

Of course, no act is without consequence. Her bag would no longer be leather, but instead a collection of plastic shopping bags; her dress and shoes would turn to worn-out sweaters; and she'd stink. It's all I can do to keep my face from wrinkling.

I bury my nose in my empty espresso cup, buying time, wondering if I should sign her death warrant. It's what she wants; she is so tired, so tired of the game, of the endless pain of watching the numbers dwindle. Soon she will be homeless anyway.

The image is fatter now, and her ankles are red and cracked

above the tennis shoes. She'll lose her dentures and smile a grin spotted with lost teeth. The scene will vanish into a pocket and she will lick her finger to pick the crumbs from the table. Her B.O. is making me dizzy.

I push back my chair. I stand. I haven't said the words. I haven't said them yet, but someone is screaming and someone is laughing or crying and it all sounds very far away, might be sound bleeding through the walls of the various theaters.

"What were we talking about, sugar?" Miss Charlotte asks, purely baffled. She is thin, she is fat. She wants me to relieve her pain. I have the power to change everything. This moment can change the world.

My world. I hold the edge of the table, reeling from the visions. My knuckles turn white as I see another past.

My father never slept with my mother. She didn't remind him of a movie star. Miss Charlotte had never made it to the wide screen, so my mother had never reminded him of her at all. Another truck driver met my mother at a bar. He'd slept with her because she was willing. Or at the very least, gullible. In this possible universe, Miss Charlotte is a happy nobody, and so am I. *What were we talking about?*

"Nothing," I say. "Nothing at all."

I edge away from the crazy, weirdly glamorous homeless lady. I can make it go away. I can make all of this go away. I can become just another guy in New York who can barely afford an engagement ring and isn't even sure he wants to be married. My kids can be sovereign to their own futures. I will be no more able to protect them than any other dad. Miss Charlotte is the key. Should I do it? Doom Miss Charlotte to a peaceful, happy, stinking death? And myself to an ordinary life, with love and despair and all of it ephemeral? Twenty words, and all places will fall mute to me, both echoes and forecasts permanently silenced. People will be as they wish to appear, without a visible past or future to betray them. I will have entered a universe in which I am not a demigod.

In which I am a fairly ordinary man.

My life would be simple as a barn.

That is: life would brim with ordinary mysteries, but I, like all mortals, would rarely appreciate them because of the constant threat of my own impending death. Mortal lives are a fulcrum between terror and boredom.

Is that a better way to live?

Is there *any* better way to live?

Miss Charlotte's bag is leather and looks too heavy for a senior citizen to carry. She sits primly, eyes cast down. Her pinky remains curled, ladylike, though her latte no longer steams. Pain and fear radiate from her snailed body until she is bright as a sun. I can see why the club kids worship her. She has owned her life in a way that few mortals ever do.

In one universe, I will walk away godlike, but one step closer to evil. In another, I will be late for an appointment, and if I get to the shop and the ring guy isn't waiting for me, I will no longer know the consequences.

Miss Charlotte looks up from her latte, and her beautiful eyes plead.

Leave Me

Her eyelashes were beginning to frost shut. Five more minutes, Chesa told herself, knowing it was foolish—suicidal even—to stay out past dark. With the back of an elk-skin glove, she rubbed her eyes until her own body heat allowed her to see again, then resumed work. She chipped away at the joint between trunk and bough, sure she was exposing truth and resonance with every tap. Feathers of ice surrounded her like a cloud of angry mites. She ignored the aches in her inner ears, her temples, along her jaw. Ignored the shuddering muscles under her thick rubber parka. A near slip, sculpting implements shooting free of the ice, and she gasped, grateful her hands had flown outward rather than taking too much and destroying the statue entirely. She cupped her hands to the ice-rimed muffler that protected her cheeks and nose from frostbite, opened her mouth and blew. Within the gloves, her fingertips were hot glass; painful and she knew from experience they were glowing red. Time to quit, no matter how close she was to finishing this crook of bough.

The wan sunlight was even now attempting to distend the shadows and darken her tiny backyard. Was trying to warn her, some might say, of impending nightfall. Her fingers creaked from the cold; she forced them to work, wiping each tool dry before wrapping all six in the oiled bearskin and tucking them into a deep pocket. She lingered over the tiny awl Mykah had given her for their last anniversary, kissed it, and placed it reverently into its apron pocket. Stood. Shuffled across the hard-packed tundra, through scattered ice chips that crunched like bones discovered by a starved dog.

Soon, heavy boots would stamp their clinging snow onto the cement porch. Too soon. She threw the bone-dry linen towel over her work, wishing she'd done more. Start earlier, she told herself. She already worked every free minute, every second she wasn't required at the plant. Work harder, she told herself, nearly dropping the keys to the padlock. How her fingers ached. Impossible to work harder or longer. She was an artist with all that entailed. The lack of common sense, Mykah would say.

She heaved on the chain to shut the thick security gate, plunging herself into premature darkness. The wall surrounding their arctic enclosure blocked the wind, blizzards, sleet—but the ten-foot cement fence shut out the sunsets along with the wolves and starving men. Yes, it was a prison sentence without hope of parole. Yes, they would quite possibly never return to the city. But they hadn't been shot in the back of the head, not yet. They lived alone, she and Mykah, and their only supervision always arrived by snowmobile. A blessing: sound travels far in cold, still air.

Still, Chesa missed sunsets. There are some things one never accepts. She once knew a woman who, after fourteen years of marriage to a procrastinator, was still surprised and dismayed when he arrived late to their dinner engagements. Another life entirely. Best to forget. Best to accept the dark skies along with the cold and solitude. She lit the seal-oil lamp without turning her face away from the rancid smoke, and long shadows leaped to life around her. A half-smile indented her lips. Shadow friends. Centered in the tiny barren yard just in front of the four rows of colored ribbons, the base of her unfinished statue gleamed in the lamp's yellow light; its smooth head covered in the thin towel, still as a willing sacrifice.

It was complete in her mind: a sinuous, reaching tree with eyes. *Leave Me,* she would call it.

In front of her was little more than a cylinder of ice. The statue was in the ice, of course; she simply had to free it.

If the commandant would grace the Superior table with it, just one feast day—when was the next one?—they could be saved from penury. Not from their life sentence, of course. But from starvation.

The tiny electric refrigerator held a modest ration of goat milk and goat cheese, warm enough within so they didn't freeze. Everything else, the meats, the canned fruits, the rare vegetable, was thrust under the snow in the tiny walled-off yard where the statue stood. Marked with colored ribbons, a civilized squirrel could do no better to organize its food supplies. A garden of frozen goods beneath the snow. She laughed at the thought of a garden. At the very idea of loam, dark and rich and stinking of the shit of well-fed animals. A fairy tale. She could not recall the last time she ate a meal without rising to her feet to shake the cramps from her thighs.

Mykah had once been an artist too. When he first heard of the sculpting contests, he threw himself into the work. She had fallen in love with his reckless use of the communal chainsaw to cut away the ice from the floes in the river. (That valuable fuel, the hungry pull of gravity, the proximity of death-as-escape.) She'd followed, useless, while he threw ropes around the massive blocks. Had thrown her arms around his when he asked for help pulling the heavy loads to their enclosure. Had worshipped his blisters in the dark, gently tracing their soft, painful curves with her fingers. She'd watched through parted curtains to see him scowling and frowning as he chipped the ice away from the form he had seen within—Greed, he called it. A sculpture made solely of arms.

The commandant asked to see it on a monthly inspection. Had nodded, her lower lip jutting out like a cliff jumper's dream. Had crossed the arms of her faded black uniform; leaned back on a thick black boot. Her nostrils had flared and streams of cold smoke had issued forth as if she were an ill-tempered dragon.

So he'd said.

"I will come for it next feast-day," the commandant had told him, just as if she were saying, "You are being fined sixty BTUs for excessively negative language," or "Mrs. Petrovich died in her sleep last night, and we are looking for someone to take her dogs." Mykah had given up a shift at the plant to insure that the statue was properly cared for when the sled came for it. When Chesa suggested she might also stay home, he told her no.

"I will ask for an extra handful of flour," he said to appease her, and then he kissed her eyes, the only part of her not covered by thick wool, skins, or rubber. "Our lives will finally improve for a while."

The money was good, the notoriety better. Neighbors trudged distant kilometers to visit and ask Mykah to describe the many-armed statue. Which way did the hands face? Were they open or closed? Were there fists? Could there have been—few asked, few dared to ask—a political undertone that, perhaps, the commandant had missed?

Mykah opened their home and their homemade hooch. He poured liberal glasses of the bitter fermented greenberry juice, grunted and wiped his mouth on his sleeve, celebrating with his newfound friends. He denied any politics, denied anything but pure creativity. "It was already in the ice," he said. It was the safest answer.

They patted him on the back and vanished when they'd depleted his new stores. Mykah fell into a deep depression from which he only emerged after Chesa traded three pats of goat cheese for an egg.

"We could live like that again if you'd work," she chastised him. "Make a new statue."

"I can't."

"What's the matter with you? Out of ideas?"

"No. The whole thing is shit. Greed? Come on. It was shit. Anyone could have done it."

"It was beautiful."

His arm tensed when she touched his bicep, so she pulled away.

"The rations—" she tried to show him. "If it's that easy for you—"

"It's not easy," he snapped. "You want rations, take an extra shift at the plant."

"I'm working all I can."

"Well, so am I."

"Maybe I'll try my luck," she mused, staring out at the frozen river in the distance. He glared at her, but he didn't forbid it.

He went back to the ice the next morning. And so did she.

***

Her first piece was more detailed than his: a black businessman and a rich white woman, both elegant in suits, both clearly in a hurry, meet at a busy intersection and hover, each coaxing the other to cross first. A remnant of her city days. How she managed to get the ice to hold the shadows of the brown-skinned man was a mystery, even to her. She'd seen the sculpture in the ice and had coaxed it forth, sometimes even blowing on the surface to melt it to the form she wanted. And the statue was good. From the angle of her calves and ankles, it was clear the woman would take the first step—bowing to tradition, acceding her female right to go first, but her eyes held apology and regret. Were she to speak, she might have said, "You have every right to go before me."

Chesa was on the morning shift when the commandant arrived for the monthly inspection. It was Mykah who was left to greet the commandant, to show the pieces, his and hers.

Chesa believed that her husband had told her everything. She took it as proof of his greater talent that the commandant had wished to speak exclusively to him. He sniffed at this, coughed his disgust. He called the whole thing rabbit shit, slammed his fist on the stone table, would have thrown something if there hadn't been so little to throw.

"You and your forced humility," Chesa said, rolling her eyes.

He stared at her.

"You don't need to put that face on for me," she baited. If anything, a fight would clear the air. At best they would make up and fall into bed together.

"Ignorant, and still she speaks."

"Stop." She put her hands on his shoulders. Tried to kiss him. "You're an artist. You have a certain temperament. I understand."

Her understanding got her shoved halfway across the hard mattress.

"You *do* have talent," she muttered at the wall on her side of the bed.

"Go to sleep," he told her. His voice was an iron shovel hitting a boulder. "Dream something."

***

What actually happened: The commandant had sniffed to see two statues in the yard. Her lip did not jut out as far as her penciled eyebrows rose.

"One is my wife's," Mykah said, though he did not explain further.

The commandant pursed her mouth, oblivious to the cold that should have chapped her features. Her lips were moist, if thin. Her cheeks glowed with spots of high color.

"Unusual work for a woman," she said, walking around the statue. "Where is the sardonic, self-deprecating humor? This piece isn't funny at all."

"If I may," Mykah began. The commandant looked sharply at him, but nodded. "My wife's statue—it's ironic."

"But not at all funny."

"No," he admitted.

"And not from our experience. It isn't current. Isn't the here-and-now. In my opinion, women do much better with the here-and-now. Your wife should make the two-day trek to visit Ana Kavininka if she can afford the BTUs. She might learn something."

"I do not know of this woman," he said, deferentially. "Is she a sculptor?"

"She won the Prize of Honor last year," the commandant snapped. "You should have heard of her."

"My apologies, Commandant."

"Accepted."

She returned to the statues, then coughed out a sharp laugh, as if realizing something. It sounded like she was trying to expel a fish bone. The sound did not raise a grin on Mykah's face. If anything, his fixed smile faltered. She looked him in the eye. "I am not the only judge, you know."

Mykah rubbed his gloved hands against his thighs. "I hadn't—"

"Then this is yours?" She tapped the other sculpture with the heel of her billy club. She spent no time wondering how Mykah had formed the ice so that it would appear to hover in the air, did not ask how he'd made the ice so thin it was transparent throughout, didn't so much as tell him it looked like liquid in motion, which it did.

"Yes, Commandant. Mine. It is called Splash."

"How much time do we have?"

"My wife is expected back any moment."

The billy club froze. "Does she not work the morning shift?"

Mykah raised his chin. "I agreed we could suffer the loss of BTUs if she took a half shift, Commandant. She was so very excited to see the judging. I expect her at any moment."

"How unfortunate." She walked back to Chesa's statue. "Tell her," she said, after examining the statue for a long while, "Tell her the eyes are good. Very good. The rest is shit, of course. She should destroy it right away, so she doesn't get the wrong reputation."

She smirked and hit Mykah's statue with her billy club. A transparent wave of ice shattered and fell to the tundra.

"You might have been someone," she said. "Imagine winning twice in one year."

***

"She liked the eyes, and said the rest needed work. But she really loved the eyes, and said I should tell you so."

Chesa covered her face with her hands, but failed to cry. The commandant was wrong. Her Street Meeting was far better than Mykah's Splash, better even than Greed. Mykah had destroyed Greed after the festival, and here was Splash, also shattered. What if it won, and there was no statue to display? How many BTUs would they lose because of Mykah's temper? They were already dangerously close to freezing every night, and the nights were growing longer.

The commandant did not choose Splash, however. Nor Street Meeting. She chose another statue, from across the river. Rumor had it that the statue was made entirely of breasts. Milk, it was called.

It was derivative, but had terrific shock value. And rumor had it that no two of the breasts were alike. That alone made it art, in some circles. Certainly, it would make good conversation at the Superior table.

They considered making the trek to congratulate the artist, but worried over the three-day journey. In the end, they decided not to go. Solidarity, they called it.

They missed the stewed prunes and the greenberry juice. Especially, they both missed the nights of warmth when they could remove their outer layers of sheep's wool and huddle by burning firewood. Firewood… that alone had made such a difference.

Chesa began to question Mykah. "Do you think they would take a statue composed only of eyes? She said my eyes were good.

Very good, in fact. Would you say I'm being derivative? I could call it Neighbors."

"You could call it The Government."

"Mykah!" She ran to the door, but of course, there was no one closer than a kilometer away. Even the electrical plant was a klick and a half down the road.

***

She began to obsess.

The last winning sculptor was a man who in his previous life had been a famous basketball player. The breasts haunted her dreams. Then, she started wondering if she'd gotten the black man wrong. Had memory failed her? It had been two years and eighteen months since she had lived in the city. She wondered if she might have had a better chance at winning if she'd used this sculptor as a life model. Wondered if Mykah would have even allowed it. How far was she allowed to go in pursuit of her art?

"Do what you want," Mykah said. "I am not making another statue. I took an extra shift in the electric plant instead. You should do the same. Art is for people with too much time on their hands. We should have a baby."

She fell silent, looking at the gray clouds that rarely lifted. The oldest of six children, she knew what a baby was like. A baby in this place? Some had done it. It didn't cost many BTUs, the government accepted it as long as the children were well spaced and began work by the age of six. It was possible that to create a live person would be as rewarding as forming one out of ice, but she doubted it. Her sculptures never misbehaved, never peed on the commandants, never spat out valuable half-chewed food, never got sick and died. A child would give her no recognition, would only slow her dreams of escape. If she had one, she would have to accept her life. This arctic ice circle. This cement box with linen curtains, this empty stone kitchen, this prefab prison. Mykah and the ice, forever.

No.

She dreamed of thrusting her hands up to the elbows in warm loam. She sculpted trees. She put eyes on the trees and hoped this would assuage the commandant. She pried Mykah for compliments.

"Do you think I'm talented?"

"Are we on this again?"

"Do you?"

"It makes no difference," he snarled, "but yes. You are. Whether you sculpt or not."

"Do you think I might ever win?"

Silence.

She learned to stop asking. Mykah ate his portion of the endless root vegetables, listened to her worries, and assured her that he loved her.

***

The commandant did not come on the appointed day. Mykah had no explanation, and no one at the plant could offer one either. Chesa stewed root vegetables in the last of the goat milk and wondered how they would live. Two days later, her off-day, early in the afternoon, three sharp raps on the front door startled Chesa. She wiped her wet and half-frozen hands on a linen dishrag and covered the laundry basket so the water wouldn't freeze.

"Coming!"

"Move faster," a male voice barked. The raps continued, in groups of three. Official business, then. But no snowmobile. Strange. She ran to the door.

A man with black hair and an angry expression stood on her doorstep. He was wearing a commandant's uniform. She stepped aside, shocked.

"Commandant Madison—?"

"Is finished," he announced. "I am Commandant Esteban."

"Come in."

"I understand you are a sculptor."

"This way, Commandant," she said, happy the contest was proceeding. A horse wearing what looked like a rubber parka quietly whickered where it stood on the frozen ground. That was new. Hoofbeats would be harder to hear than engines.

Commandant Esteban walked close to the statue, narrowed his gaze, brushed his finger across the sensual hollow between each limb and the slender trunk. He felt the tiny leaves, gently pressing their tips, perhaps testing their sharpness. He put his hands around the base, moved them up, feeling the smoothly rippled texture of the trunk. He nodded at the eyes. In posture, demeanor, in every gesture, she read that he liked her statue. Through her woolen scarf, her breath made quick puffs in the sub-zero air. Could it be? Would he choose her *Leave Me*? After resting his hand for a long time on the thickest of the tree's ice boughs, he turned to her and asked if Mykah was home. She reminded him of what he must have already known. Mykah was at the electrical plant, working his second shift.

The commandant approached her, unbuckling his belt.

***

A cord of firewood came on the next supply train. A jug of greenberry juice. A lemon. Three jars of stewed prunes. Extra rations of goat cheese and milk. A fold of salt in a paper envelope. Four eggs. Sixteen potatoes, three beets, and an onion. A cluster of wormy crabapples. A pound of white flour in a linen sack. It was more than they'd received from the previous sculpture, but then, the secret was out, wasn't it. She pushed a finger into the white powder and wept while licking it clean. Tasteless, and how quickly they would go through these supplies. And then the decision, to sculpt again, or to starve? It would be Chesa's choice, Mykah said, and he could not disguise the bitterness in his voice.

"You are talented," he whispered. "So talented. Your statues are truly beautiful."

"They don't care," she replied, her voice a small frog on the bottom of a roiling lake.

"No," he admitted. He held her so their body heat doubled.

He opened their doors to the neighbors who trekked to see them, and listened while Chesa described her winning statue to them. They pounded Mykah's back, congratulated him on such a talented wife. When they asked where she'd gotten her inspiration, she said, "It was all right there, already in the ice." No artists came to visit; no artist ever did. *Jealousy*, the neighbors scoffed. *Pride.* The exultant crowd passed around the fermented greenberry juice and squealed over the color of the lemon. When the neighbors had all left, Mykah built a fire and Chesa stared into its flickering flames. It was a moonless night and she missed the city.

1 1 7

Left Brain

At first I thought it was a learning disability, or at the worst, some sort of late-onset autism. I set up a meeting with the principal of Param's school—a coveted, progressive school with exposed brick walls, lots of hamsters, lizards, and potted plants, a rooftop edibles garden the kids weeded themselves while learning that dirt is good or that some plants have more value than others, who knows. Grading was considered harmful and violent outbursts among the preschoolers were tolerated so long as apologies were duly given along with discreet large donations.

In the waiting room, I could hear the principal on her cellphone, insisting that "incipient learners need to be free to phase through their early childhoods unobstructed by labels." I ogled the photos of her towering over the current mayor on the steps of Gracie Mansion, shaking hands with Michelle Obama, practically her twin, in the Rose Garden, then the polar opposite: hair a 70s afro, gold lamé bell bottoms, receiving a $2,000,000 check from the Foundation for Childhood Happiness at their retro disco gala.

Param had been at this school for six months and seemed happy. My meeting began with a firm handshake and ended with the principal's somber insistence that all labels be withheld until puberty.

"Give the incipient learner time to make mistakes," she cooed, ushering me out the door. It seemed to be her standard take, principal boilerplate.

The other Brooklyn moms who dropped off at 9 a.m. (a.k.a. half an hour late) dragged me to a high-end coffee shop where they suggested scientific remedies they had unearthed on the Internet or from random-sample rumor-mongering: cutting out dairy, throwing out all tech, stress-reducing yoga, gluten-free diets, noise-canceling headphones, sugarless diets (never stevia), anti-sensitivity clothing, various food allergy testing centers, and getting a complete neuropsych exam. There was a consensus about the exam. Enough of a consensus that I was able to convince Rajesh we should do it, despite the six-thousand dollar out-of-pocket cost. The neuropsychologist found nothing wrong with Param except what we could all see: He only spoke in numbers. If numbers couldn't answer a question, he would not speak.

"Would you like eggs or cereal for breakfast, Param?"

"One."

"One egg?"

"Two."

"Two eggs?"

The little chin gave a sharp nod. The bright black eyes returned to the screen where a cartoon spaceman was laughing and punching a cartoon alien back to his home planet. I made the eggs. He ate them. He took the plate to the kitchen and placed it carefully into the dishwasher. He didn't say another word.

**

At school, the lovely young teachers thought Param was adorable. They treated his condition as a quirky improv game and asked the other kids to speak in colors or in Spanish or in rhymes. The other mothers whispered that my husband had pushed Param too hard as a toddler, that math flashcards were a form of child abuse. I probably should have told them that I had been on board with the flashcards. I had enjoyed them as much as Param. It was a family treat to laugh at the wrong answers and celebrate the right ones. My husband had loved math facts as a kid and assumed his only child also would. The little boy's brain was flexible and sponge-like, and learning was hilarious and fun—a challenge to be enjoyed. Tiny Param strove to make his father grin and pat him on the head, scoop him into his arms and cuddle him, calling him little professor. For that attention, Param would have memorized anything: state capitals, ingredients in sponge cake, ancestors back ten generations, breeds of dogs, chemical formulae. It was just a game to him.

This talking in numbers, though, this was different.

***

"You look sad, Param. Is everything okay?"

Quick shake of the head. Short buzzcut doesn't even move. Eyes dart from side to side, terrified. Bubble of snot pops beneath his tiny brown cauliflower nose.

"Can I help?"

A shrug from little shoulders. Bony as a quail. Fragile.

I hand him a crayon and a piece of paper. "Can you draw what's wrong?"

He covers the page in numbers.

***

The first appointment I can get with the school's psychiatrist is six days later: a ten-minute time slot. When I walk into the room, Dr. Thaddeus P. Wall sets an egg timer shaped like a tomato, settles down with his hands tented in front of his Freudian goatee and indicates with a condolatory look that my time is already running out. I place the paper with Param's cry for help and six others like it in front of him. A page of the number 9 in various colors. A page of all even numbers in gold and black, every sixth number upside-down. A page of purple fours. A jumbled page of numbers in every one of the 64 colors from the Crayola box. No patterns on this last page, each number a different size, each unique, as if they were all snowflakes or fingerprints.

"My son did these," I told Dr. Wall. "I'm sure the principal has brought you up to speed. I want to know what's wrong with him."

"That is a very judgmental attitude to have toward a four-year-old, Mrs. Patel." I could tell he was lumping me in with every other Patel he had ever come across in his sixty-year lifespan. "Give your son a chance to explain himself."

"That's this one," I replied. I held up a page of the number one in black Sharpie. It looked like a field of thorns. It looked like a prison tally. It looked like a crazy person had drawn it.

***

I tried all the mom advice. Altering his diet. Giving away the pug. Taking him on a family vacation to the Poconos. My mother insisted it was a childhood phase and Param was just trying to keep his father's attention. My father suggested I or Rajesh spank him if it really bothered me. My older brother told me he could send me some pot to get my mind off the issue; said it would surely resolve itself soon, he should know with seven kids of his own, these things passed. My mother-in-law blamed me explicitly, said it was obviously because I wasn't cooking traditional foods from scratch—she's a bit of a stereotype and isn't welcome in my house, though Rajesh is welcome to go to hers whenever he wants his laundry done and needs both undershirts and personal vanity starched and ironed. The pediatrician—a highly recommended anti-vaxxer who thinks that all medical interventions need an acute condition to treat—got tired of my calls. The insurance company stopped covering our exploratory visits to allergists, acupuncturists, and behaviorists.

A close friend from grad school took me to an herbalist in Chinatown related to the wife of a friend of her uncle. The shop, on a winding cobblestone street, smelled of live cats, algae-covered fish tanks, and long-dead gardens. Param turned a slow circle in a room with creaky wooden floors, surrounded by jars of dried ingredients that several hours of conversation (his numbers, my words, and $600 of consulting fees) narrowed down to Panax ginseng, Reishi mushrooms, Albizzia bark, licorice root, gotu kola, and Gingko biloba. Param drank the tea with a preschooler's unhappy face. The verdict? A new page of the number two. In yellow and brown.

***

My husband taught Param math terms and sentences, taught him that i and e were also numbers. Param listened quietly but did not speak or draw imaginary numbers or constants. He paid complete attention to the long description of algebra, where X=2 or X=-2, but while he could work out the problems and give the right answer, there was no X on the page, and no equal sign, just numbers. His teachers knew that the papers with 16118113 on the top were his. This inspired Mr. Sherman to do a whole unit on codes, which only served to make Param devise a new way to sign his name: 0000001.

"I think it means he doesn't want to be understood," I told Rajesh over late night daal. Param had dropped off to sleep on the couch, the amber streetlight from Fifth making his skin look golden.

"I've been reading up on SETI and the Voyager 1 space probe. Science is using numbers as language to try to communicate with aliens. Perhaps our boy is a genius and will work for NASA."

"Did you hear me? Our boy does not wish to be understood."

"You are making assumptions for him," my husband snapped.

The boy stirred in his sleep and we froze. I was thinking, *No. It is you who is making assumptions. I am simply watching him change every day. I am simply growing frightened. It is you, trying to control his future and make him a success.*

Rajesh was first to move and to whisper again. "Perhaps aliens are speaking through him. Perhaps he is speaking to aliens. Do you think I am joking? I will show you the science. They made a golden record…"

A glass of water, slowly sipped, can calm a person. Even a person who is seriously considering calling for help. Who could I call at this point? Rajesh loves his son and only wants to help.

***

Rajesh bounced on his heels as if bringing his son a new flavor of ice cream. Param stared blankly as his father explained he was going to teach him binary. Rajesh didn't see the boy's expression when he told him he could spell Param's name in numbers. He was too busy pulling up the website on his phone.

"Zero one one one zero zero zero zero," my husband began, and looked up from his phone with a big celebratory grin.

It was as if a terrible odor had pervaded the room; ginkgo, tear gas, rotting flesh. Param's nose and eyes crumpled into a tight rose and he ran from his father. Rajesh and I stared at each other, and I knew in that moment that Rajesh was done trying.

"Go to your son," he said, pulling up his work e-mail. "Go."

I touched his arm, but he flinched and turned away.

"I said go."

***

I found him under the dining room table, quaking and sobbing. Humiliated. Terrified.

"Param," I cooed. "It's okay."

I crouched down to stroke the little boy's quivering, huddled body, and when I saw the underside of the table, my legs gave out. It had been carved with a series of fours and sevens. Sometimes in pairs. Sometime in rows. Sometimes overlapping as if one number might eliminate the other if he could just dig deep enough into the wood. Thousands of digits, hundreds of messages. This could not have been done in a week. This cry for help had taken months.

***

His teachers didn't want to change a thing about Param. They loved that he never cut up in class, never talked to the other students, raised his thumb properly and answered briefly and cheerfully when he knew he was right. His father stayed late at the office researching numeric languages, e-mailing with a trio of NASA scientists and SETI researchers he'd maneuvered contacts to on Linked In. Making progress, he said. He hadn't sat down to dinner with us in weeks, and was gone before Param was up in the morning. Progress…

Only I thought there was something wrong with Param.

"Param, say one if you agree and two if you disagree, okay?"

"Seventeen," came the quick reply. Then, hopelessly, "Eleven. Twenty-four."

***

On his sixth birthday, Param blew out six candles and shouted six with a fist pump and I posted the video on Instagram as if it were a success story. Six kids from his class attended the party and there was a cake shaped like a six. An explosively freckled Christian friend of ours chuckled with an undercurrent of real fear that 666 was the sign for an apocalyptic monster from his Bible. He was a drummer in a band that had briefly held court at CBGBs before it closed. He dragged a worried hand through his short red hair, catching it on one of his three skull rings. Told me to keep an eye on Param in June. I scoffed. Plenty of horror movies had played out that trope. Anyway, no one was writing sixes in groups of threes. The last six Param had written was in syrup on his waffle that morning.

***

The drummer's warning sounded like nonsense, but the art project that Param made after the other kids left that day was, in fact, creepy. I came into the living room because shredding silver foil makes such a chilling sound. Param had created an enormous six out of the excess gift-wrapping paper, pillows, and some jackets from the hallway, and he was covering the whole thing with foil. I told him it was a very fancy way to decorate. He didn't look up. I posted a photo of him working on the final strip on Instagram as well. With the black and white filter it looked impressive. Got lots of "likes," but I knew better. This was nothing to like.

***

I was losing sleep. My dreams were haunted by outlandish explanations for Param's condition. His right brain was slowly eating his left brain like a psychopathic sibling jealously encroaching on shared space. An exotic virus had attacked the Broca's and Wernicke's language centers of his left hemisphere, mutating the words into abbreviated symbols that his mind interpreted as numbers. An alien creature had slipped inside his ear as he was sleeping and taken up residence to learn what it could about humanity, excreting a poison that removed Param's ability to communicate except in pure quantities.

The truly frightening dreams were the ones where nothing was wrong with Param, and therefore nothing could be cured. I woke screaming from a dream where a doctor (who could have been my father) smirked as he explained that the world was too frightening and words too uncertain, that Param had made the early decision that only real numbers could be trusted. The dream-doctor then pulled the most recent MRI out of my stomach by reaching down my throat, and as I watched, horrified, he ate it. The image of the doctor smiling as he licked fingers wet with my stomach bile haunted my waking hours.

Param ate his Eggos with peanut butter and honey. He grunted in pleasure at the sweet treat, showing off the gaps where two baby teeth had been lost. "Fifteen!" he crowed before whisking the dishes to the kitchen. He had graduated to occasional double-digits.

***

I used the apps the other moms at school recommended. I subscribed to stress-tracking sites, doubled up on Pilates, started to Soul Cycle and Barre. I said no to no one, yes to every coffee date, every self-care event, every volunteer opportunity.

I went to therapy myself when it became clear that doctors were unable to help or understand what was wrong with Param—the medical consensus was to wait, to see if it got worse or better. Psychiatrists and psychologists agreed that the "interesting condition" was probably a phase. A phase going on three years now.

So I sat on an amber couch that strangers had worn out, and my feet kicked at a Persian carpet rich with otherworldly blues and greens masking a few strange dark stains. I stared at the framed prints to avoid meeting the eyes of the highly recommended therapist, a younger, childless woman who always wore Lululemon, as if my problems were keeping her from an expensive and satisfying workout. I ranted and cried about my too-demanding Ph.D.-wielding parents, vented about the demeaning nature of housework and society's inherent sexism, the demands of my job, and the problems of a society that valued the individual solely based on her productivity, whined over the thankless expectations of motherhood wherein parents were to blame for all ills, but children were responsible for their own successes, and bemoaned the lack of friends with a spiritual connection to anything but organic avocados and kale smoothies. She indicated the tissue box beside me, shifted her long legs to a more comfortable curve.

Staring once again at the framed prints of New York's most famous skyscrapers, I raged over things I didn't know I was angry about, like Brooklyn's cultural appropriation of yoga and Buddhism. Then I wept over the futility of rage in today's post-consequence society. In the end, I talked more about myself than about Param. He only held up fingers now, where he used to try to act things out. Three fingers meant hello. Five meant I love you mom, see you later. One meant no.

She nodded and said I should be more grateful that we were making progress, so I spent the next few months vainly working on gratitude.

Param did not change, but after all, as the therapist said, it was probably my problem. My inability to accept reality for what it was.

This upset me. I was pregnant again. It was an accident, a

fluke. Too much red wine at the book club I hadn't wanted to join plus not enough restraint when Rajesh got a promotion that very same afternoon. The door was closed and locked and in the morning there were ones all over the wall. Unbroken hashmarks. A field of spikes. It looked almost like art, it was so dense. Like a path to nowhere, in a long circle at his shoulder height. Param was sleeping on the floor, the marker curled in his fist, his eyes puffy as if he'd been crying.

This was eight and a half months ago. He has drawn only ones since then. He no longer meets anyone's eyes, or even attempts to communicate. The doctors have decided he is severely autistic, and left him to me and my reference books. I feed him and bathe him, I coax him to sleep with lullabies, but so far, nothing has changed at all. Except my belly. My belly keeps growing. I wonder at the wisdom of biology.

***

Last Thursday, I waddled in from a meditation session in our postage-sized back garden brushing mulberries from my eucalyptus sneakers and found Param in the middle of the floor, on his stomach, holding a Sharpie. The entire lower half of the dining room was black with his markings, but I walked right past and started up the blender full of goddess juice. My therapist says that a good mother supports her child's individualism. She says that I have to save some energy for this new baby. I have to find my center.

Param doesn't stop his manic scribbling as I pass him by.

He's focused, intent, pressing so hard that the marker squeaks on the wall. The squeak is loud and repetitive. It pierces through my calm and even clenching my teeth against the sound, I can't stop shuddering—as if I had bitten down on an eggshell, or a piece of unexpected aluminum foil. The squeak is all wrong. I duck back around the corner to see what Param is writing. It doesn't sound like the series of ones I had grown to expect.

It isn't.

In my belly, the baby kicks twice. And Param stops writing, and stares at me. The baby kicks twice again. Param slowly smiles and I am certain now that there is nothing good here. All the calm I have ever felt crumbles from me like a dried-out shell, leaving me raw and exposed. Param nods and taps his Sharpie on the dining room wall. The wall is completely covered in the number 2, and the baby kicks twice, again.

Money in the Bank

The crowd of young professionals swept into the wood-paneled elevator and David swiveled around with the rest of them like sunflowers moving to face the light. After all these years as a stay-at-home dad, he had forgotten about this natural, human, herd instinct to face the elevator doors. Nearby was a bicycle delivery guy—David had watched enviously as the young man locked his bike to a column just outside the building's vaulted lobby. In grungy black hoodie and jeans, filthy fanny pack slung over his shoulder as if conformity was beneath him, this kid was too busy looking at the address label on the manila envelope to pivot in time to the corporate dance and a matron in a suit smirked at him as if he was her own incorrigible son. David couldn't tear his eyes away. The lanky posture. The patchwork tattoos. The scraggly facial hair. The freedom. The guy's jeans had *Fuck the Establishment* blazoned across the front of each leg in paint marker. David almost missed his floor, imagining himself showing up in the apartment, wearing those jeans.

He shook himself to reality.

On his way to an interview, and admiring a bike rat's jeans? David was just nervous. Or maybe this late-April cold snap after the family trip to San Juan had done to his brain what freezing, thawing, and refreezing does to a fine halibut. Maybe having this meeting with the firm (David was unable to cross the line and call it *his* firm, not yet) was a colossally bad idea destined to ruin his life. Maybe the only bad idea was turning up while wearing a suit. But what else did you wear to meet with lawyers?

And the blue Burberry suit stirred up so many memories: the Rockefeller Center wedding of Anne's MBA friend that he'd felt so underdressed for, the corporate media job he'd abandoned just as he was hitting his thirties, Rory's christening in Maryland (also the last time they'd brought their girl into a church), Anne's annual holiday parties (those had gone the way of martini lunches; now it was just her team and a zippy new dress; no spouse-perks for him)… and here he was, monkeyed up in purple tie and starchy lavender shirt, trying to make a good impression on people he really didn't care about.

He should have stayed home and started touch-ups on the pit bull portrait. That was money in the bank, if he'd just finish it. The physical therapy Dr. Sara suggested for Rory would take a huge chunk out of their monthly budget.

Not that they kept to a budget. They just charged everything and figured they'd pay it off when Anne got a big enough bonus.

Fifty-K would help. It would help a lot.

The doors slid open on sixteen, and he faced a Middle Eastern teenager behind a desk. Maybe she wasn't a teen. Maybe David was just old. But she'd hidden a paperback under the desk and pulled out her phone the second the doors had opened. Which made him wonder: Did office policy say doom-scrolling was okay, but reading was not?

There was a violent crash from a back room, followed by a string of curses in some consonant-rich language. Not Russian, which his grandfather had spoken. Not German, which he'd studied briefly while in a collegiate, Nietzsche-induced phase of universal hatred. Probably not Hebrew, which their downstairs neighbors used to correct their children in the building's communal play space. Maybe Arabic. Or Danish. Or Dutch. Extremely angry, anyway. The black-haired girl didn't flinch. She just slid the paperback deeper between extremely thin thighs and folded her hands, looking expectantly toward that side of the lobby.

Arvyd Suzzdell, still muttering under his breath, strode from that side of the office across the large lobby and vanished behind a door that clicked open when he waved a card.

"I'm here to see the guy who just ignored my presence," David said to the receptionist, who had slid the paperback out again. "I have an appointment."

"Mr. Suzzdell will see you in a minute." She blew a tiny bubble with chewing gum and snapped it between her teeth. Chewing gum? Was that allowed? "Retro," she smiled, and cracked another bubble. She must be talking about the chewing gum. Or his tie? He was aghast at how old she made him feel. His necktie felt like a flag announcing his age. She was wearing tight slacks and a shimmery blouse unbuttoned past her pink bra line. Perhaps the bra was connected somehow to the shirt, as there didn't seem to be any danger of the shirt opening any wider. He averted his eyes, wondering how long he'd been staring and whether she'd noticed. Was it bad he had looked? He didn't know the rules anymore.

Back in his day, receptionists followed a strict dress code. He was tempted to tell Arvyd about the impression this girl had made. But correcting the behavior of others was something his father used to do. Was he seriously developing the same compulsions? Maybe middle age was actually just regression. People that broke societal rules nowadays transformed David into that tattletale Catholic-school third grader he once had been in Maryland, wanting everything to be *fair*. He rubbed his temples, aching for coffee.

"Take a seat?" the gum-chomping girl offered, but the door swung open and Arvyd saved him by waving a gesture midair.

"Oh," the receptionist said with a shrug, "Go back to the conference room."

The "conference room" was in sad shape; just an industrial folding table, a worn carpet and some metal folding chairs. The only view out the soot-covered window was of a brick wall. David sat. This fluorescent-lit room was more devoid of character than the Rockville public school bathroom where

George MacIlhenney had beat the living crap out of him and made him eat his hall pass that time in seventh grade when he'd caught the jock having a secret smoke. Arvyd would probably have encouraged his parents to sue both the MacIlhenneys and the school. And probably the tobacco company. Instead, David had gotten lunch detention for losing the hall pass and had counted himself lucky. He'd never even told his parents, but he recalled his disgust that they hadn't noticed the bruises on his arm. Or possibly hadn't cared.

Parenting had changed so much since he was a kid.

"David. Good to see you. Thanks for stopping by." Arvyd looked as if he'd just returned from a high-end shave and salon haircut; his skin glowed. This, plus his height, gave David the feeling that this lawyer was in complete control of his life at all times. Arvyd's tone was stern, professional. It reminded David where he was and why. He hadn't realized how disoriented he had gotten. The only other time he'd been in a lawyer's office was to close on their million-dollar loft—that had taken all of ten minutes, and Anne had done most of the signing. Really, they were so privileged and fortunate, even if they were drowning in debt. He thought guiltily of the easy way Arvyd had mentioned the job while their daughters played together in the preschool lobby: *Easy money,* he'd said. *Supplement your income.*

David cleared his throat, wishing he had coffee or at least water.

Arvyd offered nothing. Just asked pleasant questions that David answered without thought, as though they were both at a cocktail party and not at a job interview. Arvyd wasn't wearing a tie—the shirt was haute couture, with a tab collar and asymmetrically placed buttons of contrasting colors. And, David admitted to himself ruefully, infinitely more current, and thus, more powerful than his own old Burberry suit. Could Arvyd see the gray in his beard? Did it make him look distinguished or irrelevant? Between questions, Arvyd flicked his eyes top to bottom, which didn't help David's feeling that he was wearing the clothes of an old man.

And now the heat rose in the room. Once again, the lawyer stressed that the job was perfectly legal—a comment that immediately sent David's mind into a tailspin of worries—but Arvyd would pay cash. Five-thousand dollars, in cash, for four hours of his time. So David sat up straight and listened, like he was at a job interview for a position that was above his qualifications. Arvyd wove words into sentences that were carefully never instructions. David memorized the expertise he would be paid to exhibit. He vowed he would do whatever Arvyd needed. He owed it to his daughter. He owed it to his wife. His family would appreciate him, would be grateful. Shame trickled down his neck as he recalled lying to Anne that morning about where he was going, recalled dropping Rory at preschool and telling her a sitter would pick her up. He kicked his feet on the industrial tile floor, and wished he had worn better shoes.

Cake

Your cake knife is missing. One of the boys has taken it, no doubt.

The boys are dark, with mischievous brown eyes and brown curly hair. They look like their father, miniature versions of him with scraped knees, bruised elbows, brimming with lies. They look nothing like you.

Well.

Maybe around the eyes, when they laugh.

Your daughter is a miraculous blonde, unlike anyone else in the family. Tiny fat Buddha sitting on the kitchen floor. Strawlike tufts of impossibly white hair, blue eyes. Nude, but for the diaper. You swish a finger through the cold, cloudy dishwater, unwilling to get too wet, unwilling to finish your most hated chore, wanting that knife so you can carve yourself a hefty slice of her birthday cake as a treat to reward yourself for getting through another family breakfast.

She examines your feet just outside the spill of morning sunlight. Pokes at your red-painted toenails until you pull away from the tickle. She seems intent on finding your weaknesses, exploiting them.

Turn away from her to search the rest of the counter. You want that pink, frothy cake. Lift off the cover. Inhale the cloud of sugar. There's her name and the fat number 1 in thick buttery frosting. Cake after breakfast? Why not. Who's watching? Anyway, you baked it—Why shouldn't you eat it whenever you want?

Where's that knife?

Use the cleaver. Hack off a big chunk of pink frosted fluff. Turn back, mouth full of cake, to offer little Sarah a piece, and find her holding a handful of her own straight, white hair in her little plum-sized fist. The hair is not connected to her scalp, and it's tipped in red. The baby's pudgy face is smeared in it. It takes a moment to even register that this is blood because she's not crying. Not making a sound. Just staring curiously at the red-tipped hair. Looking at your toes. What is glinting near her other hand?

The cake knife.

Swoop down and snatch it from the floor.

She is staring in wonder at the tiny red fingerprint she left on the linoleum. The cat is sniffing at the mark; testing the blood-tipped wisps of hair with a paw.

Okay, it's bad. Not as bad as when Nicholas stabbed Benedict through the hand with a letter opener. Not as bad as when they tied their baby sister to her crib and set the whole thing on fire. But bad. Still, she's not hurt enough to cry. It looks worse than it is. But oh god, the baby, the baby!

Sarah grins when she sees you've noticed her, reaches her hands above her dark-streaked head to show she wants to be carried. Her scalp is oozing blood, but there's no bone showing. Recall from past experience that head wounds bleed profusely, but often look worse than they are. Breathe. Red-tipped hair drifts to the floor from her outstretched palm. Did they try to cut her hair with the cake knife? To scalp her?

"Boys? Boys!"

No answer. Perhaps a soft click of Legos in that part of the apartment. A footstep. Your attention returns to the baby, who is still reaching for you.

"Up! Up!" she demands.

A thin streak of red dribbles past her tiny ear and drips from her chin onto her pink overalls. The cat sniffs at the blood, tastes it. Sarah makes a beeline for the family pet, but you scoop the baby into your arms.

"None of that. We have to take you to the doctor, little one. What happened here, sweetie? Show Mommy. Let me see your boo-boo. Yucky, huh? But it's okay; it's just a tiny scratch. You'll be fine. Did your brothers do this? Who gave you the knife, sweetie?"

She smiles widely. Shows off her four new teeth. Coos "am ma ma ma am." Leaves a red smear on your favorite blouse.

You shout towards the den with its eternally closed door: *Watch the boys. I'm taking Sarah to the clinic.*

Strap her into the car seat as she stares with those huge blue eyes welling with betrayal. *You didn't protect me, Mom.*

***

Dr. Chandler examines her, fusses over her teeth, slaps her bottom, and sends her home with a little ointment.

Instead of cleaning up, the boys have used their sister's blood to draw a sigil on the wall.

"It's a protection one, mom. Not a bad one."

Bang on the den door: *Didn't you hear me say watch the boys? What part didn't you understand?*

No response.

"Nicholas. Benedict. Clean this mess right away."

They sigh. They whine. They claim it wasn't their fault. They slink away, knowing that if they fitfully return to their Legos, to their trains, you will do their work for them. Put the baby on the floor and roll up your sleeves.

It's always you, cleaning up the mess.

Fifteen minutes later, the walls are pristine, the floor shines, but the house has gone silent except for a strange scraping sound.

Run.

Find the baby playing with the cleaver. It's too heavy for her to pick up by the handle; she is dragging it along behind her by the red ribbon from which it usually hangs. The silver blade shines in the late-morning light, its edge still covered in pink frosting. Luckily all her fingers seem to be attached. The cleaver makes a clanking, clattering sound behind her as she drags it from the kitchen linoleum and onto the tiles in the hallway.

"How'd you get that?"

The scraping sound of metal on tile chills your skin. Glance at the shadows hoping to see Benedict. He's a hider. No time to really search. Give up. Sarah only learned to walk three weeks ago and is still prone to falling down.

"Akka-poo," she says, smiling. The fresh scab shows dark against her pale scalp. She plunks down on her diapered bottom and notices the fluff of frosting on the cleaver's blade. She opens her mouth for a little taste. Leans forward to the edge, pink tongue eagerly outstretched.

"No honey. Not safe."

Pry the ribbon from her hand. Don't show the anxiety you feel. She screams as if you've taken her binky. Fights. Kicks. It is as if the cleaver is working against you. Wince as the blade slices into your palm. The handle seems heavy in your hands. She is okay. She is okay. Who gave this to her? Which of the boys did this? When mothers get mad they have superhuman strength, and you are getting very mad. Conquer that cleaver and brandish it overhead. Ignore the cut on your palm. The cat hides behind a curtain. Sarah totters off after the cat. Let them go.

Bang on the door of the den with the dull edge of the kitchen utensil. No answer. *Could really use some help out here!* No response. *Hey, come out and give me a hand!*

Nothing. Typical.

Head reeling from a mix of anger drawn from the situation and relief at having averted disaster, brandish the cleaver over your older son.

"Did you give this to your sister?" Nicholas, at eight, has just begun to realize that this tiny baby might steal everything of value from him. Don't put it past him to set up an accident. "Tell me or I cut your head off."

"Come on. No way, Mom." He shrugs. "Knives are not for babies. I know that." He clearly hasn't budged from the Lego set. What is he building? A mausoleum? He never flinches. Move on to his brother.

"Benedict? Explain how Sarah got this."

Banshees are quieter. Wailing, screaming shrieking denials. "You are so stupid! You hate me! I would never—!" Dark hair flying. Hold up your palms to fend off this onslaught of noises honed on the playground. He could shatter crystal with those screams.

The den door remains closed. Hack it with the cleaver. Take satisfaction in the deep thunk as the metal slashes into the wood. Leave a gouge. Stroke it lovingly.

No response.

Return the cleaver to its high hook in the kitchen. Pour a cup of tea. Relax.

***

"Mom? Sarah's standing on the windowsill!"

Clatter of cup returned hastily to saucer. Run into the dining room. At the top of a makeshift staircase: chairs, a large crate, a stepstool, a few books...the baby is holding on to the window and waving back at Nicholas.

"Hi!" she says.

Choke back fear. The window is open. It's never open. You live on the 8th floor. Sarah holds her tiny bare foot out over the edge, as if to test the water.

"Honey. Sarah. Not safe. Hold on, mommy's coming."

Wade through the sea of tin soldiers dumped out on the floor like caltrops.

"This isn't funny, Nicholas."

A cold breeze billows the curtains into the room. Sarah sways with surprise and her fingers tighten on the painted sill. She pivots on a heel, a move she often makes before losing her balance. Run to snatch her. She burrows her face through your long red hair and into your neck and bites.

"Ow! No biting, Sarah. That hurt!" A metal spoon hits you in the back of the head. Put her down on the floor. Nicholas is laughing. The baby runs off after the cat.

"Time out for you, Nicholas. Go to your room. This isn't funny; Sarah could have been very hurt. She might have been killed. Honestly. She can barely walk. What were you thinking?"

"She likes to climb." He shrugs. "She wouldn't have fallen."

Close the window and point to his bedroom.

"I didn't open the window, Mom. She did that herself."

Point.

"I didn't do the spoon either."

Point.

"Fine. I'm going. But it's not fair."

An endless string of raps on the door of the den finally elicit a low growl. Finally. *Hey! They take after you, you know. They'd love it if you came out once in a while.* Nothing. So much for communication.

***

The front door is open. Don't panic. Try to suppress the images of Sarah ready to fall down the stairs, plummet down the elevator shaft, what have you. Dash out of the apartment to check on her. The door clicks softly shut, locking you out.

"You're so stupid, Mom," Benedict's other voice, his loving one, comes from the neighbor's shadowy stoop. That boy can hide.

"Don't use playground language in the house."

"We're not in the house, Mom."

"What are you doing out here?"

"Sarah tricked me, same as you."

"What are you talking about?"

"Sarah locked us out."

"Sarah can't reach the door handle. Don't tell stories."

"You never believe me, Mom. She really did."

"How? You tell me how a baby can unlock and open a door. Tell me. Go ahead."

Benedict falls silent. Glares. Crosses his skinny arms across his chest; the picture of an angry kindergartner copying his mother's moves.

Think about it. Wonder a little. Put together various little scenarios: the way the plastic binky falls to the floor all the time but the spoons never do. The way she loves your noisy keys and can get them from any bag. The way she looks so longingly at that cleaver when you chop the vegetables…or at the cat's metal license and shiny metal name tag on the silver-studded collar. *Wellington Cat.* Brand-new. Happy birthday, Cat.

A mother's instinct moves faster than her brain. Pound the door. Shout. Ring the metallic bell, which of course doesn't work. Of course. Collect yourself. Catch enough breath to tell your five-year old, "Benedict. Run down to Mr. Dan's office, you know the one? Run down there and get him. Third floor. Tell him to bring the extra key. Do you remember our apartment number? Can you manage? Can you do that without me, Benedict? It's really important. Can you do it?"

"Sure, Mom." He goes to the elevator, where he is absolutely forbidden to go alone. He stands as tall as he can and presses the down arrow. He soberly watches until the light goes green. The bell pings. He turns when the elevator doors open. "I can handle it, Mom. Don't worry."

Inside the apartment, there is a crash. The baby screams. Then another crash. More screaming. Pound the door. "Sarah? Let mommy in! Sarah! Please. Honey. Unlock the door! Nicholas?" Nicholas will never hear you. If there is a God, your oldest son is safe in his room, in an unwarranted time-out, probably wearing earphones while playing a video game. And what's new about screams and crashes, anyway? This sort of thing happens all the time.

There is a long silence.

Then Sarah giggles.

"Sarah?" Keep that voice cheerful as you can. "Honey? Can you let mommy in? Sweetie? Unlock the door, okay?"

She can't understand you. She's only one. Twelve months yesterday. She can barely walk. She has a three-word vocabulary. You hear a scrape as — Can it be? — the knife rack slides across the stone kitchen counter and crashes to the floor. She can move metal, that girl. All kids have a talent. Sarah's little hands clap. Just picture how happy she is with her work. "Sarah! Let mommy in."

"Kitty! Hi!"

Kitty? Sarah uses that word for any furry creature. Maybe she is after Wellington. Maybe she's just playing with her stuffed animals. Maybe.

The super shows up with the extra key. "Hey, sorry Mrs. Hawks," he says, slurring his sibilants. "I was just…you know… watching the game." He reeks of patchouli, and a lethargic smile twitches at the corners of his mouth. Snatch the keys from him and enjoy his expression of surprise. Benedict hovers, waiting to hear you tell him you're proud of him. An ungodly scream of animal agony from inside the apartment keeps you from doing so. The sound cuts off. Sarah giggles.

"Kitty." Sarah sounds happy. "Aka-bobo. Bo."

The right key on a ring of 72 is hard to find, even if you're not panicking and frustrated. Look harder. Find it, fit it in, turn it. Hear the click of the heavy bolt. Open the door.

Happy red handprints. Little red footprints tottering off to the kitchen. Entrails.

No fur.

"Sarah?"

It has to be the cat. They always start with the family pet. You can't teach them — pets — they have to move FAST to keep away from these kids. This cat lasted a long time. Longer than the hamster by far. Teething babies, wow. They just grab anything. Smirk a bit thinking of the catastrophe *that* was.

"Nicholas?"

He will be pissed. He loved that cat. But Sarah can defend herself from her brothers. That much is clear. She has a gift.

Kids. No two are alike.

But what a mess.

"Nicholas! Time out's over. Nick? Honey?"

Walk to his bedroom. The door is closed. The sign, written in marker, "no girls allowed," is curling up at the corners. Pause with your hand on the doorknob. Whisper his name, a question.

No answer. Do not open the door.

Jump when a child's small hand touches your arm. It is Benedict. He is shaking his head. Sad. He is holding something in his hands. It is dripping. It belongs to his brother. Belonged.

Cover your mouth. Turn. Run.

Bang on the den door. *Just once would you help me watch these monsters?*

Nothing. Silence.

from the leaf lore

Three hours before midnight on the night of Alban Arthan, a long stream of red taillights wound through the coastal hills of Massachusetts. This was just last year, though time can be measured in many ways. Some people believe it happened only yesterday, regardless of today. Others, who lead much stranger lives, believe it is an event still to come. Suffice to say, the event occurred—or will—and as such, it must be entered in the Leaf Lore.

So speaks Pembroke Llewellyn, keeper of the Lore.

Not far from Salem, in the midst of this glinting chain of illuminated rubies sat a couple who considered themselves middle-aged; the woman had just turned forty-seven and the man was three years older. The husband, Hollis, who was driving, was a lumpish man but a good father whose remaining crown of hair stiffly refused to turn from shoe-polish brown to distinguished gray. He stared blankly at the oncoming road, which blurred into yellow stripes and white spots in the darkness. Occasionally, he sniffed loudly and rubbed his red Brussels sprout of a nose to try to keep himself awake, or sucked air into the gap between his front teeth, intentionally wheezing. He said nothing to his wife, Margaret, who had abandoned her own attempts at civil conversation while still on the Turnpike. Neither the man nor the woman had ever heard of Druids. Neither the woman nor the man had any idea that of their union, Mother Betsey would be born. Margaret and Hollis were ordinary people in an ordinary car going for an ordinary drive in Massachusetts.

Margaret stared at her hands under the wan light of the dashboard, trying to ignore her husband's breathy noises. Oncoming headlights flooded the Lexus with a flash of white, and she wondered when she had gotten so old. Her palms were rough and callused, crisscrossed with lines, and when she turned her hands over, her wedding ring looked tight and out-of-place. The skin on her knuckles was loose, and she imagined that if she could just lift it all away, underneath there would be a new skin, and she could pretend to be young again. Maybe paint her nails the glossy candy-apple red she'd once loved. She turned to relate this thought to Hollis before remembering that she and her spouse weren't speaking; hadn't spoken for the past four hours. At her sharp hiss, Hollis turned away from the road, and asked her what she had been going to say. And try as she might, Margaret could not remember what their argument had been about.

The stars above glittered with the light of distance.

***

Three days prior to the travelers' journey, the Eldest Ovate had thrown the Ogham, and reading the order of the trees as inscribed upon the runes, had gleaned that the soul of the savior was imminently due to return. Many times this soul had walked upon the earth, sometimes in a male body, sometimes female, each time bringing great change to the beliefs of the living. The Eldest consulted no one before e-mailing the news to her closest friend, the High Priestess of a nearby Wiccan coven. This may seem surprising as Druids and Witches rarely mingle, but we live in a time of miracles. In this instance, the Eldest Ovate and the High Priestess had attended high school together in Longmeadow, and were very respectful of each other's position. The High Priestess was intrigued by the prophecy her old friend had seen and used her Craft to corroborate her friend's prediction. The e-mail she sent to the Eldest is preserved in the Lore. It reads:

TO: Martha Llewellyn <*eldest@salemgrove.etree.org*>
FROM: Sarah Millhaus <*highprstess4@salem.usawicca.org*>
SUBJECT: Prophesy

Hey Marty! You nailed it—look at what I came up with: "*Under the sign of the yellow star, a dispirited Daughter of the Soil and a slumberous Son will rekindle a lost passion, and from this Blessed Union the Mabon shall be born. The Daughter must be brought to Joy upon that night, or the unborn will perish in the bilious fluid of her womb."* Talk about corroboration! Hey, and if you want an assist with the whole Joy thing, call my cell and I'll ping the coven. Blessed Be.

***

Her friend the Eldest Ovate accepted the favor and requested a complicated spell that would bring a likely couple to Salem, where the Order of the Leaf might teach the woman to access the Awen and feel the total inspiration that is our birthright.

The Sun is our master and from him our Power descends.

It was the first time in history (before or after) that Witches and Druids had worked this closely together. Thus: Forget Not the Wicca. Though their number will dwindle as Mother Betsey leads the world to a greater awareness of the true power of the Sun, do not mock them. The seed sprouts and the seed dies. The seed will grow again. Our sisters have done a great boon for us. And Sarah Millhaus is a really nice lady. She teaches third grade, and the kids just love her.

The spell was cast two days before Alban Arthan, which the Wicca call winter solstice, and the next morning, in their six-room apartment in Boston, Hollis Affelbaum suggested to his wife a daytrip to reacquaint them as lovers. Margaret, though she cringed at his words, began to pack. The Affelbaums set themselves about trying to mend a relationship that had never been about love, but had been a civil arrangement for the sake of the children and Bostonian society as a whole. Suitcase in the trunk, they had then voluntarily shut themselves into the solitary confinement cell embraced by all of 21st century America: the family car.

In the darkness, Margaret wondered if a trial separation or even a divorce would have been such an ugly thing. A day of driving through the gorgeous coastal land where they had honeymooned twenty-four years before had rekindled exactly nothing. Just before noon, she had (out of nowhere) suggested they spend a lazy afternoon at "their" bed-and-breakfast, but Hollis had seen no point in it. They'd not stopped bickering since. When the Sun crested its highest, they stopped at the marina for an impromptu lobster, but even the pleasure of the seaside meal did not allow the couple to come to terms. And the garlic butter gave Hollis gas.

The Eldest was watching, perspiration salting her upper lip.

An emergency interfaith meeting was called, and the Wicca were commissioned to cast another spell. I, Pembroke Llewellyn, had to run to the ATM for two-hundred dollars, as the local Wicca don't take credit cards. The High Priestess, her energy still low from the previous night's ritual, directed our Ovate to an acolyte who had mastered the simple confusion-spell we required.

And loyalty won in the end. Despite the danger to her health, the High Priestess agreed to link with the acolyte and several others to increase the potency of the spell. In gratitude, our Eldest summoned the Grove's Healer, and left the High

Priestess in his competent care. Then the Eldest returned to her observations, walking with the shadows to glean what she could of the fate of the couple.

***

The trip back to Boston should have taken them only an hour, but once Hollis left the highway to avoid traffic, he had gotten completely turned around. He drove the tortuous darkness until they were both fighting sleep. In the back of his mind, Hollis hoped Margaret would consider his advice, find a hobby, a new interest, show a glimpse of the passion he had fallen for twenty-eight years ago when she first bared her freckled-shoulders on the campus of his recently co-ed Harvard. He was half-inclined to hold her hostage out in these winding back roads until she became less inexorably sour. He said none of these things, however, and more than once he caught himself drifting across the solid yellow lines. His wife was nattering on about hotels and their imminent need for one. Hollis found himself objecting. He asked if Margaret would mind if he rolled down the windows to keep himself awake. She granted her permission, although Hollis knew that cold drafts annoyed her and she would quite possibly ask him to roll them up again within twenty minutes. They suffered for each other, but only for show.

The Grove assembled and formed a circle. We left our cellphones with our coats and winter clothes, and donned the brown robes of our order, calling upon the power of the Sun to keep us warm.

I lit the first torch, in the North. I used a lighter shaped like a tree.

***

The crisp December air held promise of snow. It slapped across Hollis' well-padded frame, and he drove faster, hoping the speed would wake him. Beside him, Margaret grumbled about the cold, muttered about his navigational skills.

The car whizzed by a sign for Salem, when without any forethought, and much to his surprise, Hollis found himself promising to stop at the first hotel they saw. Margaret smiled her first smile of the trip. As if summoned, a Holiday Inn came into sight.

"How quaint," she said, breaking their vow of silence. "It's one of the old-fashioned ones." Indeed, the logo on the sign was not the trademarked cursive letters with the hovering orange flower, but rather, the chaotically flashing green and yellow neon from another decade, the old clumsy signature placard, taller than the motel itself, with its wraparound yellow arrow, and the word Inn sandwiched between two white asterisks, as if the nomenclature itself was important (or boldface!) Yellow letters instructed them to "Relax!" and poking up from this glowing mass of welcome, on its very own lightning rod was a gaudy white three-dimensional star, whose three rows of shrinking lightbulbs blinked in descending size order, as if the antiquated thing was proud of the brash Christian symbolism it evoked, aggressively glittering above an inn that always had room.

Not the modern business class signature efficiency suites, but the ancient green and yellow neon of the bygone era. Comfort and Joy. Thousands of little lights, sparkling, flashing. Happiness settled over the leather interior of the car like a chenille blanket placed by a favorite aunt. Hollis and Margaret were oddly buoyant as they exchanged the car keys for a room key at the front desk. A valet whisked their Lexus out of sight and a young bellhop with a rarely washed uniform spirited their luggage to Room 121.

The room was on the ground floor, but faced a large open field and promised quiet rest. Both man and woman were exhausted and hungry.

The Eldest watched. The Grove stood in a circle and waited. One brown-robed figure leaned to another and they exchanged names. The girl was new and the boy was eager to hook up. Their BlackBerrys were with their regular clothes; they promised to beam each other their business cards later. Someone shushed them, and they stood quickly upright.

I lit the second torch in the East.

***

Margaret tested the firmness of the bed by bouncing on it the way she had done as a child. She giggled when her stomach began to rumble. Hollis relaxed upon hearing his wife giggle, a sound he'd been craving since their second child was born with the shriveled hand. Room service was rung, and although the kitchen was closed, Hollis managed to convince the night chef to create a pair of Greek salads and send up the very last bottle of wine. Margaret listened to Hollis cajole the chef and she recalled how enamored she'd been of her husband's charismatic side, a side he'd been exhibiting exclusively at his weekend golf tournaments ever since she'd (falsely, it turned out) accused him of an affair with his glossy young secretary. Hard to bridge old wounds. A deep enough scar can kill even the oldest tree.

The assembled stood in a silent circle. The wind whipped at our robes.

I lit the third torch, in the South.

The couple ate the salads and drank the wine, reminiscing about old times when they'd both been happy. Hollis recited a poem he'd learned for their second anniversary. Margaret shook her shoulders at him, as she had from backstage at a conference where he was a too-nervous keynote speaker. Remembering old happiness allowed them to revive it, and with the red wine boosting previously dormant hormones, Margaret and Hollis fell to kissing like teenagers, tearing at each other's clothes, giddy as newlyweds.

But a chill December wind caught the flame in the South and extinguished it as smoothly as a call girl might snuff a candle.

The couple passed out on opposite sides of the king-sized bed, their union unconsummated, still wearing their shoes.

I looked over at the Eldest, swooning where she stood and relit the South torch. The Ovate caught her breath, swayed. It is difficult for us to hold power in the dark, with only the pale reflection of the Source of Life traveling the sky. Night is when the Wicca thrive, night is when the shadows live. They say that a shadow cannot be made without Light, so even the darkness is a gift of the Sun. This may be. In any case, we were given another chance. Three of the Grove supported the Eldest, rubbed her wrists with leaves still green from the summer sun. Someone handed her a bottle of Evian, and that seemed to revive her substantially. When she was back in her place, I lit the final torch, in the West. The circle was complete.

We sang to the glory of the sun, soon to return. The Eldest Ovate exhausted though she was, welcomed the Assembly. The Grove chanted our reply. Above us, the moon traveled its well-worn path around the world. In that part of the country, it had not yet reached its apex. There was still time. After quick consultation, a messenger was sent. She flew across the moonlit grass, a spark of life shooting like an endless breath across the glittering blades.

Despite the thin sheets, sticky with the scent of Pine-Sol, Margaret slept more soundly than she had in months. Outside, our source of power was behind the earth, illuminating the Wiccan Moon to its full radiance, eclipsing the stars with reflected light. As the sky was cloudless, the face of the earth was outlined as if painted with a thin coat of white fire. Where there were lakes, the moon swam in them. Where there were forests, the moon seemed to be tangled in the branches of the tallest trees. Where there were mountains, it looked as if the moon could be approached and touched.

The message was intoned.

Margaret was having a dream that was making her smile in her sleep; in her dream, she had successfully courted a seven-million-dollar check for the museum, was accepting an honorable title from her children, a plastic surgeon and a famous painter (the disabled child's fame was her favorite part of the dream), and someone was knocking on the door. Knocking. Knocking. Margaret woke up startled and disoriented, but soon the piney smell of the bedspread reminded her that she was in a cheap hotel not terribly far from her home and that the man in the bed beside her was only Hollis. Her bunched-up nylons had cut the circulation from her left leg, which tingled and pinched. The knocking which had awakened her paused, and then continued. She threw on her skirt, buttoned her blouse. The knock was decidedly human, and was coming from the window, not the door. Thump-thumpy-thump-thump. Pause. Thump-thump. Over and over.

Margaret twisted around until she could see Hollis' lumpy body in the dark.

"Hollis," she whispered.

He did not respond.

"Hollis, get up. Someone's knocking on the window."

Hollis had passed out face up on the bed, reminding Margaret of a hibernating bear. His baggy stomach rose and fell steadily, his legs were spread wide to no good effect, and his right foot dragged the dingy carpet. Although his mouth hung open, Hollis' breath whistled through his nose. His eyelids twitched and then his left hand jerked as if someone had slapped it.

The knocking continued.

Margaret shook her husband by the shoulder. He was still wearing his jacket, but his pants were down around his knees. She vaguely remembered removing his tie to kiss the loose folds of his neck. She hated that tie with its loud pattern of yellow golf balls. It trailed across the carpet like a spent balloon, reminding her of their earlier cheerfulness.

"Wake up, you old jackass!"

Hollis stopped snoring, but did not wake. This did not particularly alarm his wife. Red wine always rendered Hollis insentient. Margaret shook her husband so that she could later truthfully say that she'd tried to wake him and failed.

Across the wide field, the Eldest Ovate blessed the children of the assembled, called for prayers and petitions. Some wanted to get their kids into Montessori schools with long waitlists. Some wanted healing for their parents with Parkinson's or liver cancer. Others merely prayed for serenity and an upturn in the economy. There was a lot of political grandstanding, as there always is. Further thanks were given for the aid of the Wicca, and blessings and a cheese pizza were sent to the Ovate Healer in vigil over the High Priestess (who had not returned to consciousness since the Linking). A chant was raised to Margaret, to help her trust the messenger.

She was Called.

***

Feeling self-conscious, Margaret slipped out of her navy

Ann Taylor pumps and picked up a shoe for defense. It was either that or the curling iron, and the curling iron had a long annoying cord. Not a good weapon at all, she decided.

She inched her way to the window. The cheap carpet felt like sandpaper through her nylons. She was afraid she might be in shock. It was as if someone else were controlling her mind.

Thump-thumpy-thump-thump.

It was too ridiculous to fear—this shave and a haircut rhythm. Probably some local kid trying to spook her. She was oddly at ease when she pushed open a crack in the blinds.

A blue eye stared right back into her own.

That did it.

Margaret leaped onto the bed and took Hollis firmly by the lapels of his jacket.

"Hollis, Hollis, *get up*. Get up!"

His head lolled as if he were the Raggedy Ann she'd nearly decapitated once on a playground trying to prove a point to another mom. A small thread of saliva spun its way down to Margaret's wrist from her husband's lips. She wiped it away as if it were a spiderweb. Hollis mumbled something that sounded like, "Fix it yourself."

Margaret snatched up the phone to call security. There was no answer. She dialed the front desk; no one picked up. Panicked, she called Room Service, and the phone just rang. Ten, twenty times.

She placed the receiver in its cradle.

Thump-Thump.

Margaret circled the room in her stockinged feet, picking things up and putting them back into place. She plugged in the curling iron and set it to hot, just in case, and feeling more and more ridiculous, returned to the window, her mouth scratchy with the taste of spent wine. Know your enemy, she thought, heart racing. Just a child playing a prank. The window was barred. She felt safe. Sort of. She took a deep breath and prepared herself for the blue-eyed gaze that she now knew would be waiting. She opened the blinds and the messenger waved.

The Eldest Ovate smiled. The Grove exploded in cheers. Someone started up "Who Let the Dogs Out," and it was all chaos from there.

***

Standing before the window in the neon light of the motel sign was the sweetest, most angelic girl Margaret had ever seen. Although it was the 21st of December, the girl wore no coat, but instead was dressed in coveralls and a long-sleeved thermal shirt, like a farmer child. She was only about fifteen and the nest of mouse-brown hair on her bare head bounced as if it had just been washed. Her lips looked puffy and moist in the strange combined light of the moon and motel sign; her mouth turned upwards at the corners as if the girl had never learned to frown. Each time Margaret looked at her face, the child waved her hand in joyful greeting. Despite her fear, Margaret eventually smiled in reply. The girl had a pimple on her chin. Margaret was unable to be afraid of a girl with a pimple.

Margaret tried to shoo her away through the window. The girl waved again, still smiling; the brown curls of hair giving her a youthful energy that Margaret suddenly craved. The teen beckoned, and Margaret turned to her husband. He snored.

Adventure requires boldness.

She looked back at the visitor who again gestured: "Come out." There was nothing threatening about the child, but she was beginning to glance about as if she were late or perhaps worried about something. The girl wore white tennis shoes, the kind one might have bought in a Woolworth's before the drugstore vanished from the face of the earth, and her toes had worn through the canvas. Margaret sighed: the girl's toes were painted licked candied-apple red. Her red.

Margaret left a note for Hollis, saying she'd gone to tell the concierge that the phones were down. Then she pocketed the room key and opened the door.

***

"Hello Margaret, I'm Elizabeth. Betsey, for short," the child announced instantly, and she grabbed hold of Margaret's wrist. Her grip was surprisingly strong for such a thin young woman.

"Do I know you?" Margaret responded, dumbfounded. The moon was high, but all Margaret could see was the vast empty field behind the motel; no landmarks, no vehicles, nothing that indicated whence Betsey had appeared. For her part, Margaret was not dressed for a December night, yet she felt cozy, as if she'd been wrapped in old furs. Even her bare feet were warm. She wriggled her toes, feeling the hard pavement of the parking lot catch the nylons. The runs tickled as they laddered up her legs. She giggled.

"Ours," the Grove thought as one.

The white crowns of Queen Anne's lace made long shadows in the moonlit field, and on the distant horizon, Margaret could make out several dark shapes moving in erratic patterns around what seemed to be a large fire. But Betsey did not let go of Margaret's wrist, and Margaret found herself walking slowly away from the peripatetic figures and towards the edge of a dark grove of trees. A fine thing, or the Wiccans might have used her energy to fuel their Solstice sacrifice, and then where would we be?

"Will you dance with me tonight?" Betsey asked.

"I have not danced since my own wedding reception, and that was long ago..." Her voice trailed off. Margaret hadn't seen her undress, but the flash of white among the tree trunks ahead of her was a naked wraithlike girl scampering about in the winter-dead grass laughing and whistling a tune that reminded Margaret of a commercial she used to like for a coffee she never drank. Margaret's fingers wrapped around the fabric of her blouse and even as she clutched the buttons tightly closed, her stout woolen traveling skirt, the blouse, her support bra, her ruined pantyhose—even the leopard print panties she had inexplicably dug out of the back of her bottom dresser drawer for the trip—all melted away as if they were lemon sherbet left in the sun. She looked down at herself. Sagging breasts. Stomach pitted as a golf ball, the bellybutton a spelunker's dream-crevasse. Her thighs were rough and jiggly. Her pubic hair too long, too straight, too coarse, too gray. Her toes were gnarled as baobabs and her feet were mapped with several mountain ranges of blue veins.

She sat down in the dirt and started to cry.

Her thighs spread like vast white sausages on either side of her. She could not look at herself.

"You. Are. Beautiful." Betsey's voice shimmered from the darkness between trees. "Nature's activities can be seen upon your skin."

"The hell I am. I've had this body my entire life, whatever-your-name-is, Betsey, and it is spent. Over. I wasted it. When I was your age I spent hours in front of mirrors, admiring nature's activities, as you call it, dreaming of what I'd do when I had a woman's body. I used to try to guess where the curves would be. Where the wrinkles would appear, how the hair would look. A woman's body. Well, here it is. Ugly and fat and fat and ugly.

"But where did the girl-body go? That's what I want to know. I can no more see that adolescent firmness now than I could predict the furors of old age when I was a teenager."

"Can a tree remember its growth from an acorn?" Betsey replied, appearing at her side, a wood-nymph, a dream, impossibly young and lithe, perfect in her lack of age, perfect in her lack of fear.

Margaret shook her head, angry. It wasn't an acorn she wanted. It was the sapling, whipping in the wind.

"Then dance!" Music rose around them as if from the trees.

At first her feet would not move. She had rooted in the soil, those great thighs of hers sending out shoots into the dirt seeking nourishment. But as the voices rose around her, Margaret rose. Her knees creaked a little, her back resisted, but soon she was upright. The winter weather did not touch her. Ten minutes later, she was dancing: breathless and panting. God only knew how far away her clothes had gotten. She was in the middle of an unknown forest in the middle of December, heedless of the pine needles, the sharp sticks, the stones, not to mention the broken glass, the aluminum cans, the newspapers, the rotting banana peels, and the rest of the debris that humanity peppers over its planet. She danced. She rolled her head from side to side, kicked up her knees like a chorus girl. She threw her arms over her head and shook her shoulders so that her breasts flopped from one side to the other like old shoes tied together by a ratty lace. She never wondered if what she was experiencing was real or a hallucination, if it were dangerous or meant she had gone off her rocker. She simply hopped and jumped and thrust her chest and elbows out until her eyes leaked. She slapped her thighs and her flabby ass, and she nodded her head until her hair came loose from its tightly pinned bun and whipped her in the eyes. Then she laughed. There was music in her head: a happy, Celtic sort of music composed mainly of voices. Distant voices making music like flame. She opened her mouth to sing along and found that she knew all the words, that they were words that her mother had sung to her and her mother before that. In the crib. During storms. Whenever she needed strength and hope. Wordless words made of sunlight and falling petals. Words made of singing and joy and trees and roots and earthy shrieks of delight.

She touched the Awen.

Briefly she felt the icy grass sting the bottoms of her feet, the December wind graze her face and breasts and back with its nails. She looked around clear-eyed, and terrified, and cold—and was returned to her bed.

She would never remember how.

And in that bed, she pressed her cold feet to Hollis' legs and his shriek reminded her of something fierce and fun, but she ignored that feathery memory for she found her husband's body warm and fully willing. Afterwards, they clung to each other like drowning newlyweds and Margaret murmured that she'd had the strangest dream in which she thought she'd danced naked. Her husband fought to suppress a rising belch and failed. The stink of half-digested salad dressing, salami, and old, sour wine flooded their cheap hotel room.

She caught his eye and they both burst out laughing. It was so human: to make love, to belch, to laugh. So infinitely human.

That huge belly laugh reached his toes and hers—and unbeknownst to them--to those third, as yet undeveloped sets of cells that soon would grow to be the toes of the Mabon: who in her time will lead us as our Mother Betsey, Keeper of the Way. Wait and see. Druids may seem quaint and weird to you, but ten, twenty years from now, you too may be leaving your PDA in a pile with your day clothes, and donning a coarse brown robe, waiting to touch the Awen that is your birthright and your joy. For at the very moment that Hollis and Margaret joined in laughter in that ratty Holiday Inn on Route 22 in Salem, the Eldest Ovate knew that the prophecies were fulfilled.

And even though it was very early in the morning, the Eldest Ovate asked me to text-message our Healer and ask after Sarah Millhaus' progress. He replied with a smiley face that by noon, the Wiccan would be hale as a lumberjack, so we all agreed to meet for lunch at that darling little seafood place that just opened up on Route 1A, for, as you well know, the High Priestess is an absolute fiend for steamers.

Big Bad

Years after our argument, Hunter found me on Facebook and apologized. He wasn't studying theology anymore, but after his initial message, sent scanned images of paintings he'd done in his free time. Crucifixes viewed from above surrounded in long robes with demon tails. People in prayer around fires. Moldy bread and wormy fruits. Within the following year of e-mails he spoke of love three times. Twice he broke up because the women would not convert. The third one, he decided to marry and convert later. All were virgins.

    I had promised him when I was his babysitter that I would never turn away from him. It was after I found him trying to revive a maimed tabby cat with a spell after finding her on the side of the road, closer to dead than alive. The spell never worked, so I stood by his side and helped him dig the shoebox-sized grave and say goodbye to the creature in the hot Texas sun. There was a lesson to be learned under the distant cloudless sky, the prickly mesquite, and baked into his tousled bare head: Magic was terrible and real and promises should be kept.

He was always more interested in magic than in hard work, and because of this had gotten swept up in a terrible cult in high school. When I used my grandmother's magic to bring him back to the right path, he was initially grateful. It was only later that he said these words had caused our initial argument and the years of distance.

I was glad to have him back, even if he thought magic was fairy tales. Even if he had become a born-again Christian. Even if he thought I was going to spend eternity in hell for my ways.

Perhaps that was why I neglected to tell him that Elson and I had been too busy since moving from Texas to New York City for me to spend any time with my grandmother's books. When I felt ready to discuss my choices, too much time had passed, and it felt strange to admit that I had wandered away from the path that had divided us.

So, like very ordinary people, we exchanged Facebook messages and liked each other's posts. And then Hunter fell in love this third time, and I cast stones out of sheer curiosity, and nothing worked properly: I saw only a stick creature and a broken river.

I told him nothing.

When Hunter asked for help in ring-shopping with a page of website links, I suppressed my qualms in order to rake him for more details on the bride. He would only say, "Our belief systems mesh." And I couldn't tell if that was irony, shorthand, or some new way to avoid Facebook knowing too much. He posted pictures, and I was surprised to discover Robin had just turned twenty-one. Hunter was pushing thirty.

One of the photos had a caption, "goodies" and I couldn't tell whether that was a code or literal or something that younger people say about each other. The photo was in the Great Piney Woods and showed Hunter in a flannel shirt unbuttoned to show a little gold cross, pretending to chase Robin with a toy hatchet, and Robin in a flowing white gown pretending to run away. Her feet were bare and her dark hair was loose around her shoulders. Her dress was stained all around the hem as though she frequently played dress-up like this in the woods.

She was as much younger than Hunter as I was older. Beside her the little kid I babysat once upon a time looked like a man. Until that moment, I'd never realized I think of Hunter as a little brother. A very, very little brother.

Then a miracle occurred in my life. Married ten years, my gynecologist told me the Pill was the cause of my migraines; so I got off it. The migraines went away, replaced by heaving morning sickness. Elson and I were, after initial alarm, greatly overjoyed.

I eventually called Grandma to share the news.

"Well, good luck," she said with a little sigh. I could hear the ice clinking in her drink. "I wonder if you're strong enough to be a mother." The rest of the day, I slept on the couch, afraid for my baby. Barely the size of a lemon, by the time she saw daylight, the world would be slavering, eager jaws wide, waiting to crush her to a pulp.

Twelve therapy sessions later, I started smiling when I told people I was expecting. I felt the euphoria of innocence again, delight of the unknown. I phoned Hunter with the good news. He seemed distracted. His fiancée had postponed the wedding for the second time. Instead of talking about my growing family, we talked about Robin.

"She's gone back to living at home." His voice sounded shaky.

"Maybe she's not ready to be married. She's pretty young."

"I want you to meet her and decide for me."

"Decide for you? Hunter?"

"Honestly, I don't know. I proposed and she said yes. But I don't know."

Plans were made for them to visit us around Winter Solstice.

***

There was no snow that December. The winds bit one day and caressed the next. Blue-lit menorahs and white Christmas lights speckled the windows of local apartment lobbies, and plastic Santas with glowing bellies sprang up beside the omnipresent blue Virgin Mary in fire escape balconies. Elson assembled the crib and we pushed it from corner to corner, wondering how we'd ever find space for a new human being in our cramped apartment. I had grown pendulous breasts and a round belly that outsized them six times over. My fetal daughter kicked me in the ribs when I ate spicy food, but otherwise just squirmed, reminding me of a cat trapped in a tight blanket—all sharp bones and nowhere to run. I still had two whole months to go—so I gave up waiting for the baby.

Hunter and Robin's arrival date was sooner and far more solid. I cast the stones on a bored afternoon and got the sticks and the broken river again, and an animal. I thought I heard a howl and got up to close the window we had opened because the steam heat made me swelter with my large belly full of future human.

***

A weird e-mail surprised me the day before they were due.

Robin's dad is coming too. He's got a business trip. See you tomorrow. Hunter.

Elson pulled out the air mattress and wondered aloud if our semi-engaged guests would sleep in the same bed, since Hunter was so obsessed with virginity. Laughing, I suggested the couch as a chastity suite.

***

"Nan? Hunter here. I'll be alone. Mr. G is taking Robin back to his hotel because she's not feeling well."

He arrived an hour later with apologies from his fiancée, who had some sort of stomach cramps she blamed on some organic sprouts she'd eaten at the airport. Hunter's eyes looked tired. His facial hair had filled in. While he talked, I pictured the boy I'd saved from drowning, that heavy diaper. The rebirth of pulling a child from the deep end of the pool. The amused mockery from my grandmother, "Now he's yours, you know. You've changed the course of fate. You've scrambled the story; it's all wrong now. You'll never know what happens 'til it happens, more's the pity. So much harder this way."

Hunter was making excuses for Robin's absence: "She says it's not contagious, just wants to stay with her pops."

"How can she know? Maybe it's a stomach bug."

Hunter changed the subject. "You look amazing. Look at that life form!"

I hugged him and we laughed about the fact that my belly was in the way.

***

In the morning, Hunter was sitting on the leather couch looking glum.

"She's feeling worse. She can't hold down water. She says it's reflux."

"I know all about reflux," I said. One of the nightmare side effects of pregnancy. Battery acid in the throat. I tried to keep my voice light. "Not contagious. Let's go visit. I want to meet this girl of yours."

"I have to buy pineapple juice," he said. "Her father's orders. By the way, don't call her Robin, her dad prefers Red." His face darkened. "I hate that name."

"Let's go," I said, pulling on his arm.

***

She opened the door with a cheerleader smile, squealed, and threw her arms around me. I backed away. She wore a pink T-shirt with a bright white daisy in the middle. "I'm so glad to see y'all!" she said, and her voice was a cheerleader voice to go with the outfit: pitched too high, stridently happy. "It's just awful to be in this room all alone."

"How do you feel?" Hunter asked, his arm going protectively around her shoulders. She shrugged him off.

"Careful! The door will close."

"Don't you have a key?"

She hesitated for less than a second. "I don't know where it is," she chirped. "Come on in."

The shades were drawn to dim the room, the television blaring a Kevin Bacon movie. Sheets had been hastily thrown back to cover the large bed. I looked at her, alarmed, but she was already chattering away about how much she adored New York City and how *lucky* I was to live here and how much *fun* we were all going to have if she ever felt better and how *great* it would be to take in a Broadway show. Hunter opened the juice bottle for her, and she dutifully poked in a straw, but at the end of half an hour, she had still not lowered the table of the beverage, nor would she touch the croissants or sweet strawberries that room service had delivered to her nightstand in a basket.

I needed protein, suddenly, ravenously, I wanted red meat, craved it. Needed something juicy to chew full of iron. I wanted a French dip or steak and eggs. The larger the animal the better the sacrifice. I told the room I had this craving, and Robin told us to go on ahead to lunch. Her father was coming back at 12:30

and had asked her to stay in the hotel room until his return. I suggested we go to the hotel's café, leave a note for her dad to join us. She didn't think it was a good idea to disobey him.

Hunter's phone rang and it was uncannily Mr. G, in the lobby, wondering if Red had gotten the pineapple juice.

"I am coming up," he announced. "Ready or not."

One bed, I thought. *One bed.*

Robin didn't rise when her father entered the room. She poked at the sheet entwining her ankles. Mr. G was a lean, angular man, balding, with a carrot-nose that seemed vulpine. He was wearing a three-piece suit, cheap but flashy, and shook my hand without meeting my eye. His first comment to his daughter was, "I see you've straightened up a bit in here," and I wondered at the way he made it sound both suggestive and a barb.

I was staggered by a series of images of him cornering her and telling her she had to obey him because he was her father. I was haunted by subsequent visions of her turning her face away from his. Of her eating nothing as punishment for both of them. For all three.

"We're going to lunch at the hotel cafe, Daddy," she said, and her eyes were overly bright. "Give me your room key."

Her father took her by the shoulders and squeezed and I saw how skeletal she was—holding out her hand for the key, she looked like a sixteen-year-old.

"You don't need it, sweetheart," he said, smiling broadly. "I'll wait for you to come back. Don't be long. You wouldn't want to tire yourself out."

I stood there as if my jaw had come loose.

"I need to make some calls," her father continued, his voice pompous as if he was closing billion-dollar deals. I wanted to scoff at him, to break the spell. To announce that making calls was nothing special. To pop the self-important bubble in which he lived. Before I could draw a breath to speak, he mysteriously added, "I might just show up, though, so don't do anything I wouldn't do."

That was distracting. I wondered what *that* might be.

Mr. G did not join us for lunch, and by the end of an hour, Robin laughed easily at Hunter's jokes, and chattered about New York and how exciting it all was. I couldn't help but think, *You've seen nothing but the inside of your hotel*, but I kept my mouth shut. Over the course of the hour, she'd pursed her lips against the rim of the pineapple juice so often that half of it was gone, but refused to eat even the skinny bread sticks that lived in the center of the bread basket.

"I can't," she said, smiling as brightly as the daisy on her shirt. "I wish I could, but I just can't."

She vanished into the bathroom a moment later.

"I was thinking," she said when she returned wiping her lips, "our kids are going to be cousins!"

I wondered how a person with such an obvious eating disorder would go about dealing with the distortions of pregnancy. I ate five square meals a day, not counting snacks and had already gained thirty-six pounds. My breasts weighed more than most summer melons. Did Hunter really love this woman or was he punishing himself for his true desires? Had I caused this by turning the story inside-out?

***

I finally saw her put food into her mouth. Elson and I took the younger couple to a chic Tribeca restaurant where we were sure to see famous people (as if on cue, an unshaven John Stewart made an appearance, child in tow), and Robin begged the glossy waiter for a bowl of chicken broth. This wasn't on the menu and he fumbled and fussed as foolishly as a peasant before a priest in an old tale, but after a while he went back to the kitchen and fetched her what she wanted. She glowed as she pointed at the golden broth with the spoon:

"Oh, how delicious this soup looks!"

"All the better for you to eat it, my dear," Hunter replied.

"Oh, how delicious the soup smells."

"It certainly seems that it wants to be eaten, my darling."

She dipped the spoon into the shiny surface of the golden liquid, delicately disturbing only one of the parsley flakes.

"Oh, how delicious this soup tastes!"

"It's why God gave us eyes, noses, and mouths, my dear."

She ate four spoonfuls and then went to the bathroom. I looked across the table at Hunter, who had now spent several nights alone on my air mattress. He was rigid as a tree; a little gold cross at his neck glinted as it caught the halogen light.

"She's leaving tomorrow," Hunter said. "Going home with her father."

"But you guys were supposed to stay a week."

"I know."

He had nothing else to say. The girl smiled too much. There was only one bed in the hotel room. This dinner was the first time she'd left her father's side. He wanted to save her, but Hunter was in over his head.

She returned with a glowing report of the bathroom décor. It seemed she'd never seen an orchid before—and in Cook, Texas, perhaps she hadn't. Desserts arrived and she devoured a gooey piece of chocolate cake with raspberry sauce. I watched her lick frosting from her fingertips and wondered if I'd ever see her again.

In the morning, she left with her father, his arm a huge sausage over her tiny shoulders. Hunter went on to the airport, returned an hour later, holding a pint of rocky road and two plastic spoons.

"You okay?" My tongue, cool and creamy from the melt of chocolate chunks.

"I guess."

"You didn't know she had an eating disorder?"

"That's not the whole story."

"Okay, but it's part of the story."

"God will take care of it."

I wondered what it would be like, to travel through life expecting to be saved all the time. The baby kicked. I took Hunter's hand and put it on my belly, watched amazement lift the gloom from his eyes.

"It's really alive in there." He pulled his hand away and looked me as if I had changed color. Wonder tinged his voice.

"It's a baby."

"Well." I laughed. "It will be as soon as it's out here with us. Right now, it's like a mystery inside of a bag."

My spoon snapped in half as I dug for deeper caramel. I loved Hunter for bringing ice cream to me. For thinking of me. For letting his babysitter become a surrogate sister. We both needed family, the world was a dense forest and family the only path to safety.

"Do you think I need to do anything?" Hunter said as we reached the bottom of the carton with our spoons. "About Robin, I mean?"

"I don't think you can take her away unless she wants to go, Hunter."

"Yeah," he said. "I really hope she wants to go. I think she does, most of the time, but then sometimes…"

The baby kicked again, and I patted my stomach like a Buddha. I reached over to take his hand again—a man's hand, I noticed. The fingers were long and thin, an artist's hand. His nails were bitten as low as they could go, and near his wrist there was a little tuft of black hair that had not been there the last time I had seen him, when he was a teenager and I was a very young adult. I stroked the tiny patch of hair and placed his lovely hand flat on my belly again where a knee or an elbow scooted across the smooth roundness from one side to the other. He yanked his hand back.

"Freaky. There's people in there."

We both cracked up laughing.

"Nan," he said, "you're going to be a great mom."

A Rose

Sanjid al Bashachra lifted the glass rose to his face. It was as cold as the wrath of Allah, but a hundred-hundred's times more rare. The rose had no scent, and as he held it, it wept real tears upon the brown sands of the desert. Sanjid had never before traveled to the wondrous City of Cairo, and until he beheld this rose, it had seemed to him impossible to surpass the magnificence of the great pyramid in whose shadow he now stood. Sanjid trembled at the beauty in Allah's world and blessed His name. The glass merchant winked a merry eye.

"Come, son of the sands," he said, "purchase this trifle for your beloved. No woman alive has seen such a lovely, tragic flower."

"Indeed, wise merchant, I have as yet no beloved," answered Sanjid, for he was an honest fellow, "but I am held in enchantment and will pay whatever price you ask for this rose, which must be unique in all the lands."

The merchant, sensing an easy mark, rubbed his hands in delight. "Three golden dinars and it is yours, as you seem a lover of beauty. And yet," the merchant's voice dropped to a menacing growl, "you must also purchase this magic coffin in which to carry the sad flower. I fear if she sees the full light of day, she will cry herself to oblivion." Indeed, although the light of the sun was flaming upon the desert, in the shade of this hidden alley, darkness was all but complete. Yet the crystalline rose captured the distant light of Allah, and in its heart, it sparkled. Sanjid clapped the merchant on the back, for he was eager to complete the transaction.

"I will, good friend. How much do you ask for the case?"

"Ah," the glass merchant whispered, "it is precious to me. No less than four-thousand gold dinars will allow me to part with the coffin in which this rose must lie."

Sanjid threw up his hands. Four thousand gold dinars equaled all the wealth in his father's caravan. Yet, Sanjid felt he must have the rose. It bit his palms anew as he transferred it from one hand to the other.

"Very well," Sanjid said to the merchant. "I will bring this wondrous rose to my father in his tents. If he approves the transaction, you shall have your four thousand. If he disagrees, however, you must consent to the return of the rose."

"Certainly," agreed the merchant, triumphing in his heart (for he was an evil, treacherous man), "but if you fail to return the rose to me intact, you will forfeit your life, your caravan, and all your lands in Baghdad. I will await you here after the sun crests the high pyramid on the morrow."

"If this is Allah's will, then let this bargain be sealed," responded Sanjid, and scurried off into the burning sun of Egypt to show his father the wondrous weeping rose formed of this new glass called ice.

***

"Holly? Snap out of it. Hey, Cigaret-girl! Have you gone flooey or something? The picture is half over, and you haven't sold as much as a mint."

Holly jerked her eyes away from the pack of Camels she was holding.

"Oh, Penny!" she squealed, "Gosh, you gave me the willies. Pen, listen, I just dreamed up the most adorable story. It's a real powder-puff. And what a flick it'd make. Set in Egypt! Valentino to play Sanjid and I don't know who'd play the glass merchant…"

"Look, peach, I don't wanna crab your act, but save it for later, won't you? Big Moe'll flip his lid if he sees you zonked there like a sot. You know you can't sit on the Palace steps. If your dogs ache, hide in the ladies' like the rest of us. Big Moe's on his way and you'd best be on your feet when he gets here or he's liable to can you and me both."

"That old Moe's a rotten louse. He can go fan a duck for all I care," Holly said. But she got up from the velvet steps of the cinema entrance—dealing with Big Moe on the solitary was not the way to deal with Big Moe.

The way she told it, Holly had left Philadelphia primarily to get away from being bossed around. She had big plans, and her

Pop was standing in the way of them. He was a missionary—from him, she'd heard enough about wrong-doing to last three lifetimes. If her Pop ever found out she'd started peddling cigarets to the wallys at the movies—well, he would take it big.

But her Pop wasn't so holy, neither. Oh no. He was a bit of a swellegant towner—old Philly just wasn't posh enough for this particular minister's daughter. He'd packed her off to New York City to live with her recently widowed Aunt Josephine, intending that Holly use some of the culture she'd picked up in finishing school, not to mention Aunt Jo's prestige, to meet a proper young man. See, the old man had started thumping Bibles so that he could be assured that his daughter would come home with a Rockefeller on her arm; it was a trade-off, even-Steven. In the Reverend Pristmire's mind, God was in his debt.

Little did he know that his sister had gone wild after her husband kicked the bucket. Holly's Aunt Jo surrounded herself with artists and flappers. She was a night bomber. Matter of fact, Jo was thrown in the clink the very same week that her young niece showed up on her doorstep. Jo'd been caught soaked in silly water at a gin joint on 23rd. But she'd got out free just as quick as she'd got nabbed—Jo had friends. Heavies. Friends with big cars and bigger rolls of dough.

It was Aunt Jo that'd suggested the name change. "Miss Violet Pristmire" would never do in the City. "Holly Bibble" was ever so much cleverer—and shocking too—considering her Pop was a man of the cloth. Holly loved it. More men had been charmed by that name than she could count. Holly had Jo to thank for everything: Jo had bobbed off her long dark hair, taught her where to rouge her knees, basically given her entire image a plucking-up. Before she met Jo, Holly had known nothing of the art of queening.

These days Holly could coo with the rest of the pigeons. She never sold many cigarets, but she made a killing in pocket money. Her stories were her special gimmick. Men adored them. Holly could make up a topper on the spur of the moment, inspired by whatever little thing. Today, it'd been the picture on that box of Camels. Often it was the new cigar boxes, or the posters of the latest DeMille. Or the particular tilt of a lady's head. Or her mink. Holly often dreamed of owning a mink. And soon she would.

"You girl, what the Sam Hell are you doin' lollygadding about? Screwy dame. Get'cher feet movin' an' yer mouth talkin' an' yer fingers sellin' or this carpet won't be the only thing that's worn out 'round here." Big Moe's booming voice knocked into her. Holly jumped in her skin. Her idea had better work.

Just at that moment, the doors opened for intermission and a crowd of swanky folk swarmed the lobby. They grumbled like a handful of precious stones, the diamonds scratching the rubies and emeralds. It was time. She'd been planning this moment for weeks. Holly threw down her tray. Mints, candies, cigarets, matchboxes, cigars, and loose change bounced across the carpeted lobby. The money be damned. This was her night and she was ready.

"I don't need you or this damn job," she announced. The crowd murmured its approval while Big Moe and Penny gasped. Holly flounced towards the exit with the smoky crowd, drawing energy from their startled elegance. She was an event. A hit. The crowd was grateful to her.

"I've had it with you, Moe Ginsburg. You can't treat me like a dog. Hell, you're so mean even a dog wouldn't stick around here for long. I'm sick of slaving for you and this cinemagogue." Holly tossed strings of insults over her shoulder, wishing they were long strands of pearls. She skipped down the stairs, her square heels clicking as she reached the parquet floor of the outer lobby. There, she stopped and turned. She tore off her faux French-maid's apron and flung it at the House Manager. A ripple of admiration circled out through Holly's audience.

"I quit, you big mug!" Holly's exit line was pronounced as if it were the final line in a melodrama. At the foot of the stairs at the end of the canopied entrance, a glossy black Packard waited for her and her adorable stories with open doors; from within, a single wisp of cigar smoke trailed into the sky. Holly waved at Penny as she got in, the seams of her stockings crooked for the last time in her life.

***

"What are you thinking?" John asked Susan. Her blue eyes had unfocused and a soft smile had drifted across her face.

"Nothing," Susan answered, snapping herself out of her daydream. "Nothing much." She sat in the passenger seat of the 1928 Packard. The couple had been test driving the antique car for nearly an hour, through cornfield after cornfield. Susan liked the feel of the soft leather interior, the old-fashioned look of the dial-filled dashboard, and she'd been caught daydreaming about a crazy '20s moll named Holly Bibble and her Mob connections. Susan wished she could be as bold as her Holly.

There was nothing to look at out the window but dull variations of weeds and dirt. The tall, blonde man in the driver's seat had not spoken for several minutes. Susan tried to muster up the courage to ask him why they were still driving through farmland. The arches of a McDonald's loomed on the horizon.

"Hey, are you hungry?" John asked Susan.

She stared at him.

"We just ate," she said. "You brought me out here to talk. You said you couldn't talk in the city. I didn't come here with you to eat at any stupid McDonald's in the middle of a cornfield. I told you we should stay in Topeka, but no—you had to drive out into the country." She turned to look at the endless highway, her right hand resting lightly on her belly.

"But Suse—honey—okay, here goes—oh, shit. Please don't be mad, darling. Please?" The McDonald's flashed by, and the cornfields returned.

"What the hell is going on with you, John?" Susan could no longer look out the window. Beads of sweat trickled down John's square jaw. He made a motion as if he were chewing, then opened his mouth to speak. The words rushed out in a single stream.

"Well, sweetie, see, we ain't ever gonna be able to go back to Topeka. I stole the car. Felony. It's worth thousands. We're movin' on." He turned briefly from the road to open the glove compartment. A ring box rested in the otherwise empty hole.

"Oh, John!" Susan's big blue eyes grew big as teacups. John had not changed, not one bit. She tugged at the wisp of her long blonde hair which fell in front of her shoulders. On the other hand, at least this time he was bringing her along.

She reached for the box and opened it. Sparkles filled the car as the Kansas sunlight hit the diamond.

There was a moment of tranquility. Neither John nor Susan moved. The ring glimmered. The cornfields rolled beyond the windows of the car.

"I'll do it," Susan finally said, "but once the baby is born, you've got to get a regular job, agreed?"

"Agreed."

Her left eye twitched with skepticism, and she used the lacquered red fingernail of her ring finger to separate her curled eyelashes. Words rushed out of John's mouth, past his perfectly white teeth, as if he had been trying to stop them.

"Suse, I'm no good. Will you really marry me?"

"Of course, stupid," Susan chuckled. "No need to make a big production out of it. I love you, John-boy. Now get me and this baby to Canada, before I change my mind."

***

"Americans are not like that at all!" Ramon said in Japanese, "You make it sound like a soap opera." Akiko blushed and lowered her eyes. She still could not believe that this broad-shouldered Spanish man spoke her native tongue so fluently. He was coaxing such secrets from her heart. She could believe even less that she was enjoying revealing them. She had invented these characters for her own amusement several years ago. She now inked their tragic drama into comic strips with the calligraphy set that her dear mother had bought her once for the Celebration of Dolls. There were many stories of that ilk buried in the silk folds of her mind. Stories of the Americans, Susan and John, and their adventures. Many of them graphic and sexual. These would be unfolded later, after more sake or perhaps plum wine when he tired of the rice liquor. Ramon was laughing. Not at her, she hoped. But he was laughing, at last. His laughter mingled with the tinkling of the wind chimes. Her story had been a success. Satisfied, Akiko again gave him her full attention. He was speaking with that sensual accent. She had never heard Japanese spoken so mellifluously.

"Americans are far more dull, and not nearly as pretty. Most of them are horribly fat, or as bony as fish," he was explaining, noting privately that her figure, while feminine, was neither fleshy nor skinny. He could happily pluck this lotus blossom. His eyes leveled to the neck of her kimono. He focused on her breathing. It was heavier than before. He let his dark Spanish eyes caress the curves of her arms. His gaze then traveled over her entire body, head to toe. One toe was in a white sock, separated from the others by the thong of her sandal. He removed the sandal, the sock. He sucked her toe. She moaned. He lingered on the toe until her graceful undulations caused him to look up.

It was time to peel the skin from the pulpy fruit, she thought, unwrapping her obi. As the material wound out, away from her perfect almond-colored body, she looked at Ramon's little

Emperor, who, if she was not mistaken, was rising to meet her.

And still, the thick silk wound away. Slowly. Accompanied by music from a plucked instrument. The lights had faded to red. Soon, Akiko's breasts would be revealed. Soon. Ramon's eyes saw nothing but the silk winding and falling to the floor around his spring flower.

***

"James Forrest Dickinson!" his mother's voice shrieked at him. "What are you doing in your brother's room?" Jimmy fumbled with the remote, not wanting to miss any of the good parts, knowing he was already caught. He hit the mute button, and the strange, smooth language vanished. But he could still see the action. Brown tits under red light. That Ramon guy was about to make it with the Japanese lady.

Wendell's T.V. had cable. Channel 56 was the International Porn channel. You didn't need to understand it to figure out the story.

"Oh shit, oh shit, oh shit," Jimmy said to himself. He was in for it. His mother loomed over him. She snatched the remote control from his fingers.

"Turn that crap off," she howled and although she was the one holding the remote, Jimmy fell towards the T.V. in his eagerness to comply. He grappled with the power switch. The beautiful and forbidden brown breasts vanished from his sight. Not before his mother noticed them.

"I told you never to watch that channel." She smacked him

across the ear with an open palm. "What's wrong with you, you little pervert? You're not even fifteen years old yet. You hardly even have a prick of your own. Christ, Jimmy."

Jimmy cowered, hating himself for not standing up to her. His face burned from the knowledge that she was right. He had seen the pricks on this channel. His was not like that at all. He lifted just his eyes and peeked at his mother. She was still mad.

"Jim, Jimmy, what am I supposed to do with you?" she asked. "I suppose you're going to turn out like your good-for-nothing brother?" He didn't think she really wanted an answer, so he stayed silent. His mother grabbed his arm above the elbow and pulled him upright. It usually hurt less if he let her move him around, so he followed her down the hall to her bedroom. He felt his thighs tremble. She was going for the belt.

The belt was the only thing that his father had left behind.

***

"Rubbish!" Miss Carthwight tore the leaf of paper from her black typing machine. She wadded the half-written story and tossed it into the dustbin with the others. Samuel, her Siamese cat, sauntered towards her desk. She leaned to scratch his ears.

"Good puss," she purred, "I can't concentrate today. The bloody thing keeps turning into a domestic situation. Or Oedipus. Last time it was Oedipus. What am I to do with this commission, Sammy? I don't write violence. Tomfoolery, I say. Perhaps I need psycho-therapy. What do you think, pussikins? Ridiculous, right?" Samuel leapt to the first shelf of the bookcase.

Miss Carthwight pushed her spectacles higher up on her nose.

"Do you think it's because of Uncle Willie, puss? I shan't ever be rid of him, shall I?" Samuel licked himself.

"Don't sneer, you terrible beast, or you shan't have cream." Miss Carthwight looked at her calendar, noted the day, and sighed. "Shall I jot down some ideas, and then why don't you and I have some nice soothing tea? There, Sammy. Would you enjoy some tea? Good puss. I expect you'd be very fond of a biscuit." Samuel turned his back. His owner sighed. The grandfather clock ticked in the corridor.

Miss Carthwight poised her hands above the keys of her typing machine and began tapping. Ten minutes later, she heard a loud crash. The grandfather clock had fallen face forward and now rested at an angle like an old canoe. Splintered wood, shards of glass, metal dials, cogs and pendulum parts were scattered across the floor. A rounded knob from somewhere was still rolling in a slow circle.

An elongated musical phrase played on an invisible violin. It had come back.

"Here, puss," Miss Carthwight called, frantic. "Sammy!"

But there was no answer.

"Oh not the poor puss," Miss Carthwight said, but she knew that the curse had taken her cat from her as well. First her sister, then her mother, and now—after the requisite ten months and ten days—her cat. She stood from her work, took up her cane from its resting place next to the desk, and hobbled over to the clock. The cat was lying on its side, and if not for the bloody streak across its grey fur, Miss Carthwight would have thought

Sammy was asleep.

"Pussy, pussy, pussy," she repeated, in a daze.

***

Kara looked out the grimy café window at the red neon lights blinking "PUSSY PUSSY PUSSY" across the canal. It was dark, after midnight on her last night in Europe. She hadn't been out this late in her entire month of travels. Most of the hostels had an eleven o'clock curfew, and even if they didn't, she'd had nowhere to go, no one to accompany her. Most of her midnights were spent asleep, curled up in a small circle of light with whatever book she'd been reading. Kara knew herself; she was doomed to be meek as a bug. This café was a mere city-block away from the notorious red-light district of Amsterdam. Kara could see it from where she was sitting, the red lights reflected in the dark water of the canal, beckoning her, and yet she for the past hour she had stirred her cold coffee, unable to work up the nerve to set foot across the canal, much less to truly explore.

Red, red, red: in every language, the color meant stop. She finished her coffee and rose from the table, leaving a generous tip. If she were to die or be captured and sold as a sex-slave, she wanted to be remembered well by her last waiter. Kara wound a path through the small tables towards the public bathroom at the rear of the café, and stepped into a filthy room with a single hole hewn into the floor. She could almost see the stench rising out of the hole. She locked the door. Her eyes watered as she pulled the traveler's wallet from between her breasts. A single ten-guilder note was left. That was all. She transferred the money to her jeans' pocket, left the bathroom and gasped for fresh air. Her waiter was serving a glamorous Latina at the table she had just vacated. Kara wished she could wink at him as she left, sexy, sultry, so he would be sure to remember her, but the waiter never took his eyes from the full Spanish lips. And anyway, Kara figured she would have lost her nerve at the last minute. She ducked her head and backed out the door.

On the street, a bicyclist nearly ran her down and she flattened herself to the brick wall to avoid him.

"Sorry," she told the man, who spat foreign curses at her, got back on his bike and rode off. "Don't be a mouse," she told herself, and she looked at the reflection of the flashing lights in the dark canal. But she was a mouse, she'd always been a mouse. She was afraid to cross the canal. She turned the other way, leaving the red light district behind.

The cobblestones hindered her as she walked. The soles of her practical leather shoes twisted as she stepped on the odd flagstone. She passed a cathedral and considered for a moment that it might be sensible to stop and allow this church to be her final destination instead of the hotel. A couple was making out on a park bench in the shadows. Kara tried not to watch but they were so drunk they were losing their balance. The boy was about sixteen and had his hands awkwardly twisted into his girlfriend's clothing. One hand was down the front of her too-tight pants, the other under her sweater. His elbows knocked together with jerky motions while his girlfriend squeezed his crotch and made noises that sounded like a seal's bark. As Kara giggled, the young couple toppled off the bench.

They didn't even notice, except to take advantage of the more comfortable prone position. It filled Kara with longing, which disturbed her. Her stomach still curdled when she thought of Troy's sunburned face snarling those words at her as she lay vulnerable on the boat-patterned sheets beside him: cock-tease, he had called her, and she had only been twenty. It was no wonder that each subsequent time, she had allowed less and less contact, until her boyfriends began to call her "the nun" and finally stopped calling altogether. She felt her lip tremble. It seemed as she got older, her standards had risen, and men all seemed too ordinary, too similar. It was difficult to want to give herself to someone who wouldn't appreciate it, who was more interested in his company going public than in her slight fear of spiders, or her extreme fondness for eating walnuts from their shells. As trite as it seemed, she wanted her first time to be a moment she would remember forever.

At the same time, 31 was too old to be a virgin. "Saving herself" was no longer a victory, now it was an embarrassment. She had denied herself with the overeager boys who would have left her pregnant at eighteen, denied herself for religious reasons until she was twenty-four, looked for Mr. Right, looked for Mr. Fine-for-Now, briefly considered women, and finally given up altogether. On her thirtieth birthday she had considered throwing herself in front of a car, but dying a virgin seemed to be more shameful than living as one. It didn't matter. It shouldn't matter. She was a sensible, mature adult. Her time would come. Still, she lived in fear of dying in a freak accident before she could be normal, like everyone else.

She walked on, wondering why the trip back to the hotel seemed so long. A bookstore and a church looked oddly familiar. The orange streetlight illuminated yet another straight cobblestone pathway, lined with black bicycles. She walked along another brick wall, crossed another bridge. She turned right, then left, and found herself standing right in front of the café where she'd just spent an hour over cold coffee. The Latina woman was applying copper lipstick while her waiter hovered with her change. Kara had walked in a large circle. It was as if Amsterdam was giving her a second chance.

"Now or never," she told herself, adrenaline pumping. "Don't be a mouse." She took a deep breath and crossed the bridge towards the flickering neon signs.

Soon she could see the display in the first of the red-lit windows. An obese black woman was pressing rolls of naked flesh against the window pane. She wore two gold bracelets on her wrists and a metallic sarong around her waist which had the effect of aluminum foil on a burnt Christmas ham. Her bare breasts looked like crushed prunes. She lifted her arm and wound her fat fingers into the curly black hair in her armpit. She seemed to take pleasure in unnerving the passers-by. When she saw Kara staring at her, she licked the window glass with her purple tongue. Kara blushed and hurried onward.

"Perfectly legal," she reminded herself. "Don't be a mouse."

Each subsequent window held a new woman. Some were beautiful. Some were so thin that the black circles under their eyes looked solid. The next window that Kara stopped at framed a lovely Asian woman who held a German Shepherd on a leash. The Asian woman beckoned her, pointing at the striped cushions of her sofa, causing Kara's heart to skip a beat. She walked swiftly onward, wondering how her life would have been different had she gone inside.

It affected her, imagining Nancy and her mega-sized diamond ring and brassy I-used-to-be-high-clearance attitude shying away from the woman who had made it with an Asian whore. She walked straighter, swifter. Her ankles didn't wobble so much. She met the eye of many of the women in the windows. She smirked at couples with their arms intertwined in jealous fear.

In the heart of the District, the streets were well lit and crowded, although the crowds were mostly male and mostly drunk. The men propositioned Kara as if she were expensive. It amazed her that they found her more desirable than the professionals in the windows. As she walked by the neon-lit clubs, doormen called to her, "Live fucky-fuck. Come in! Free for you, pretty woman. Free fucky-fuck." The cajoling doormen reminded her of the night-manager at her hotel who had told her that his five eligible sons were all doctors....

And then Kara realized that she was lost. The streets all looked familiar, the women all looked the same. Each turn seemed to take her deeper into the world of commercial sex. Doormen recognized her and pushed their sales harder. Shopkeepers asked if she wasn't too shy to buy. She lost her lovely new posture, lost her speed. She wandered along the cobbled streets, her feet beginning to seriously ache. The prostitutes began to look old or bored or both. She felt horribly visible, as if someone were about to throw a cloak off and reveal her as the only virgin in a six-mile radius. She grew terrified. The men in the streets became irritating with their endless and uncreative offers. She was meat. She turned left, then right, then left again. She wanted to crawl into her little hotel bed and forget about her fantasies of becoming someone else for a night. She wanted safety. She craved it. She turned right, then left, and ended up in front of the Asian woman again. Her German Shepherd barked and Kara hurried by, horrified that she'd even considered the earlier proposition.

A hand touched her arm. She jumped. The mouse was trapped.

"Excuse me, miss." The voice was made of thick milk. She turned to look for the source, but no one was behind her. She trembled.

"I'm sorry to spook you. I mean no harm." The voice was male and came from a shadowy alcove near a blazing advertisement for Dr. Feelgood's Sex Toys. Kara considered running away, but there was nowhere to go.

"Okay," she said brusquely to the shadows, "come out. Show yourself."

"It's just, you look lost, miss," the male voice said. "You walk by me thirteen times this evening; I count." *Thirteen,* thought Kara, *there's luck for you.* She said nothing.

"Miss?" the voice was tentative. "If you like, I take you back to hotel. Where you stay?" Kara's mind raced. If she told him where she was staying, he'd know where she was staying. If she didn't, she might never find the way back to her hotel. Thirteen? Could she have been that lost?

"Miss?" the voice came again. "I promise not hurt you."

That's reassuring, thought Kara.

"Miss?"

"Yes," Kara answered, swallowing hard. She felt like she was about to dive off a cliff into a pool of water that was either deep and cold, or shallow enough to break her neck. "I am staying at the Schluessel Hotel. I would be grateful if you'd show me how to get back. I left my map there. And my husband. He's a big man. A black belt in karate. Six-four. He is a policeman back in the States." She knew her lies sounded stupid, but she didn't care.

"Your trust will be rewarded," the man said and he stepped out from the shadows. He was a foot taller than she had expected, towering over her in an orange sari and flat leather sandals, and his black hair had been shaved into a topknot. He was holding a white plastic bucket filled with assorted cut flowers that sloshed when he moved.

Kara took a step away. The tall man gently shook his head and seemed to float back towards his hiding place. In the shadows, his orange sari seemed to vanish, though Kara could faintly hear the slosh of his bucket.

"Miss," he said, his disembodied voice taking on an irresistible tranquility, "you are not forced to follow me. It is your choice. Your opportunity. What are you missing in your life?" The words resonated off the strangely empty street. Opportunity. It was what Kara had hidden from her whole life. In safety, she had missed opportunity. Kara pictured Nancy, Troy, and the rest of her coworkers huddling around her lunch table as she told them about the humongous cultist who had saved her from the evils of the red light district. Her life suddenly sounded exciting. All she had to do was allow him lead her back to the hotel. She emerged from her shell of fear.

"Do it, mouse," she told herself, and she discovered she was feeling bold.

"Okay," she said aloud, "I'd like your help."

"It is my pleasure," the cultist said, hefting his white bucket on his hip. "Follow me."

The couple reached the hotel within the hour. At the door, Kara pulled the ten guilder note from her wallet and offered it to her guide.

"Thank you," she said.

The cultist looked up at the waning moon, as if for advice.

"I cannot accept material good without giving something material in return," he said. His voice was hypnotic. "Allow me give you a flower."

Despite her protestations, he searched the flowers for his deepest, reddest rose.

"Many hide in there," the cultist said. "Many of you." He grinned, and Kara found that she really liked his smile. He offered her the rose. She could taste its attar as she inhaled. Its petals brushed her lips and she knew that no one at work would ever see her again. She invited the cultist upstairs.

The rose was still full in the morning.

Virgin Flight 244, Chicago to Heathrow

In airborne darkness, the pain of birth. She grabs her neck just above the locket and feels the pointy head of a small creature emerge from the hollow in her throat. It gives a soft bleat. Reeling, she holds the small idea in her hand, amazed that such a bloody, furry thing could have come from someone like her. Palms cupped, she shields it from the sleeping passengers nearby—like any newborn, it nestles deeper, afraid of the world. Her throat bleeds onto her pale yellow blouse; despite the splintering pain of speech, she whispers eager reassurances.

"I will nurture you. You'll grow."

Her husband shifts; her reawakening sends fingers of lightning to rouse him.

"What is that?" he demands.

Her hands open into a tulip. He peers in and draws back sharply. He has seen only its helplessness, but that is enough.

"Yours, I suppose?"

She nods, mute, as the delicate thing casts its swollen black eyes at them.

"You're bleeding, you know. It looks bad."

The intercom pings a captain's announcement. The thing bleats in response, loudly, fearfully. People are starting to shift in their sleep. She holds it close. It bleats again.

He reaches across her and twists, silencing it.

"I'm doing you a favor."

Sadly, she's already bled to death. He opens her locket and finds only himself.

Someone offers him a drink which he accepts, and when the flight attendant walks by with the flimsy white garbage bag, he has many things to put inside.

Acknowledgments

Thank you for reading this book: If it weren't for you, it wouldn't matter that I wrote it.

I want to have coffee with everyone who has ever said a kind word to me along the way, and coffee is on me for any of you who told me to keep writing. This includes everyone at Columbia, whether you liked my writing or not (you made me), and all the authors who passed through the Pen Parentis Literary Salons, because hosting you and interviewing you reminded me that while writing is joy, publishing is mostly tenacity. I must of course thank Max Talley and Angela Borda for dragging me out from under my cozy rock, and must also specifically thank Emily Speer Ryan, Emily Pulley, Fiona Soltes, Jim Charlton (yes, I still remember you helping me get to St Petersburg), Tim Carroll, Greg Truman, and all of the members of Cake — you all get special prizes because you keep agreeing to read my rough drafts no matter how many of them there are. Arlaina, I appreciate you for holding my hand through the baby years and Christina, for taking up that mantle through the teen years and beyond. Kathryn Okashima, thank you for the copious intelligent conversations and the emotional safety net. This book goes out to you and to Lawrence, Erazmas & Zina—you keep believing in me despite all evidence to the contrary, and that deserves more than just words, but words are all I have.

—M. M. De Voe

Biography

M. M. De Voe is an internationally published fictionista who once danced for the Pope and later ran away with a group of jugglers. Her writing has won over twenty awards. Columbia University Writing Fellow, MFA under Michael Cunningham and Matthew Sharpe. She also co-wrote a dance musical called *R/Evolution* with composer William Moulton, produced Off-Broadway at Tisch School of the Arts. Founder of the literary nonprofit Pen Parentis, a process described in her memoir/productivity guidebook for writers who are parents, *Book & Baby* (first place in the 2021 NextGen Indie Awards in the writing and publishing category). Inaugural member of the Lithuanian Writers of the Diaspora Forum. She lives in Manhattan.

Follow her on Twitter @mmdevoe.
Subscribe to mmdevoe.substack.com.
Author's website: mmdevoe.com.

Borda Books
www.bordabooks.com

Hurricanes & Swan Songs, April 2019

Dames & Doppelgangers, October 2019

Delirium Corridor, December 2020

Silver Webb's All Hallows' Eve:
The Thinning Veil, October 2021

The Fifth Fedora, Fall 2022

A Flash of Darkness, April 2023

Santa Barbara Literary Journal
www.santabarbaraliteraryjournal.com

Volume 1: *Andromeda,* June 2018

Volume 2: *Cor Serpentis,* December 2018

Volume 3: *Bellatrix,* June 2019

Volume 4: *Stardust,* November 2019

Volume 5: *Wild Mercury,* September 2020

Volume 6: *Saturn's Return,* June 2021

Volume 7: *Oh, Fortuna!,* August 2021

Volume 8: *Moon Drunk,* December 2022

Volume 9: *Space Sirens,* June 2023

Made in the USA
Middletown, DE
28 May 2023